Together Always

TOGETHER ALWAYS

Mimi Barbour

Sarna Publishing

This is a work of fiction. Names, characters, places,

and incidents are either the product of the author's imagination

or are used fictitiously, and any resemblance to actual persons
living or dead,

business establishments, events, or locales, is entirely
coincidental.

Together Always

Vicarage Bench Series – Book 7

Contents

Contact Information:
233

Dedication

This book is dedicated to my Russian friend, who I know as Edward. He sent me a birthday greeting last year and requested one of my Vicarage Bench Books for his book club. They were readers who enjoyed the stories and had no possible chance of getting a paperback for their library. As soon as possible, I sent him one, along with my sincerest regards.

Move ahead to the beginning of the new year and my 85-year-old mother said how much she would appreciate a post card from Russia with the Olympic games emblem on the front. I wrote to Edward with this request and my wonderful friend not only sent post cards, but he also mailed a notebook and some special Olympic stamps in his parcel.

Because I'm worried for him and his family during these traumatic times in his country, I wanted to send him a special gift. Together Always is dedicated to him with much love and hope for the future...

Praise

Hilarious! – "I have absolutely loved every one of the Vicarage Bench stories! With mystery, suspense, conflict, humor, and romance flowing artfully together, they make a fun read. Of course, what better way to develop compassion and understanding in each other than to "walk a mile in their shoes"? Ms. Barbour is far from the typical slow and boring romance writer."
~ Reviewed by J.P. Riley

Freedom to Choose – "For me heaven is reached when the spirit leaves the many encumbrances of the body and experiences absolute freedom. Grace loves life, but dies from an insipid brain tumor. Vanessa hates life and dies because of her horrid childhood. Yet the spirits of both women come together in one body by choice, although throughout most of the book it would seem that Vanessa would rather be any place else other than where she currently resides.

It's family that binds these two souls together, one because she never dreamed she'd actually have a husband and son to love and be loved in return, and the other, because she can't let go of the child that loves her unconditionally, such a love she'd never known before. Ms. Barbour weaves a story of struggle and pain, but resolves it with acceptance and wonderful compromise. Hope springs eternal! Great read!"
~ Reviewed by Flojo

Great Story! – "From the moment when I started

reading this book, I could not put it down. I enjoyed the story and each character. They each felt so real! Then, the end was perfect for the story. It did not disappoint me."

~ *Reviewed by Zelly Rodz*

Also author of...

~*~*~*~

The Vicarage Bench Series
— Spirit Travel at its Best! —
She's Me (Book 1)
He's Her (Book 2)
We're One (Book 3)
Vicarage Bench Anthology (Book 4 – Books 1-3)
Together Again (Book 5)
Together for Christmas (Book 6)
Together Always (Book 7)

***

Angels with Attitude Series
— Angels Playing Cupid! —
The Angels with Attitudes Anthology (Books 1-3)
My Cheeky Angel (Book 1)
His Devious Angel (Book 2)
Loveable Christmas Angel (Book 3)

***

Elvis Series
— Make an Elvis Song a Book! —
She's Not You (Book 1)
Love Me Tender (Book 2)

***

Vegas Series
— Action–Packed Thrillers! —
Vegas Series – Complete Boxed Set
Partners (Book 1)
Roll the Dice (Book 2)
Vegas Shuffle (Book 3)

High Stakes Gamble (Book 4)
Spin the Wheel (Book 5)
Let it Ride (Book 6)
***

Undercover FBI Series
— Popular & Compelling! —
Special Agent Francesca (Book 1)
Special Agent Finnegan (Book 2)
Special Agent Maximilian (Book 3)
Special Agent Kandice (Book 4)
Special Agent Booker (Book 5)
***

Holiday Heartwarmers Trilogy
— Truly a Christmas favorite! —
Holiday Heartwarmers Series
Please Keep Me (Book 1)
Snow Pup (Book 2)
Find Me a Home (Book 3)
Frosty the Snowman (Book 4)
Love of my Life (Book 5)
***

Mob Tracker Series
— She's unstoppable! —
Sweet Retaliation (Book #1)
Sweet Justice (Book #2)
Sweet Resolution (Book #3
Sweet Endings – (Book #4)
Sweet Faith (Book #5)
***

Other Titles
I'm No Angel
Hotshot Cowboy
Big Girls Don't Cry

Christmas Runaway
The Surrogate's Secret
Mimi's Mix (Box Set)
'Tis the Season (Box Set)
Hearts, Flowers & Romance (Box Set)
Red Hot Divas (Box Set)
O authorsLove, Christmas (Multi-author Box Set)
Unforgettable Romances (Multi-author Box Set)
Kiss Me, Thrill Me (Multi-author Box Set)
Sweet and Sassy (Multi-author Box Set)
Unforgettable Heroes (Multi-author Box Set)
Sweet Heat (Multi-author Box Set)
Unforgettable Christmas (Multi-author Box Set)
A Christmas She'll Remember (Multi-author Box Set)
Snowflakes and Christmas Kisses (Multi-author Box Set)
Unforgettable Valentine (Multi-author Box Set)
A Valentine She'll Remember (Multi-author Box Set)
Unforgettable Suspense (Multi-author Box Set)
Unforgettable Danger (Multi-author Box Set)
Unforgettable Trouble (Multi-author Box Set)
Unforgettable Weddings (Multi-author Box Set)
A Wedding She'll Remember (Multi-author Box Set)
Enchanted Romances (Multi-author Box Set)
Sweet and Sassy Brides (Multi-author Box Set)

***

All Mimi's books can be found on her Amazon Author
Page:
OR
Website: http://mimibarbour.com

Chapter 1

Bury, England, 1977

Lucas watched his wife's arrogant neurologist stride into her private hospital room. It was the same chamber where he'd sat beside the iron bed, hearing the continuous beeping of the life-giving machines attached to her lifeless body. It seemed like he'd spent forever in this dreary room.

Unconsciously, the muscles in the pit of his stomach cramped in fear of the results he expected. From the sympathy etched over his patrician-like features, Dr. Hoven had bad news. Lucas braced himself to begin his act.

As if to demonstrate his competency, the physician lifted Vanessa's hand to take her pulse and then leaned over to check each pupil. He hummed under his breath the way doctors do when they want to look efficient.

Finally, he spoke. His voice was like that of a funeral director: eerie and full of fake compassion. "Mr. Knight, you know why I asked to speak with you today?"

Lucas nodded and furtively crossed his fingers.

"I'm afraid the news is bad, sir. We've conducted several

extensive tests and the results are even worse than we expected. It looks like we'll be forced to take your wife off life-support within the next few days. She's deteriorating so quickly, there doesn't seem to be much hope left."

Solely for the benefit of the man standing in front of him, Lucas assumed an anguished expression. So desensitized had he become over the past horrific months, it was difficult for him to allow any realism to seep through his protective barriers. Bitter sorrow, his true emotion, had shadowed him for months. "I was afraid of that, Doctor. I've sat here every day this week watching her get worse rather than better." The sigh he allowed to escape lasted seconds longer than normal. "She's slipping away from me." He reached for her pale hand and held it next to his face, his performance improving after being in constant demand.

The white-coated practitioner, commiserating through the tight smile he shared with Lucas, leaned against the bedframe and continued. "Frankly, I'm surprised. I'm sorry to have to admit this, but it's almost as if she's fighting to die. Her multiple injuries were grave, certainly, but repairable. After she came through those earlier operations so well, we rather felt we'd performed a miracle. Her remaining in the coma has surprised us all."

Lucas watched the slender medical man whose military-like bearing and frosty personality made him quite unapproachable.

"Unfortunately, since she has no brain stem reflexes or pupil response, we've had to accept the inevitable. Without brain function there's no hope."

Lucas closed his eyes. Hold on, man – just a little longer!

Drunk and dangerous, Vanessa had driven her car into a ravine full of water and had been submerged until a passing motorist came to her rescue. Lucas had thanked the Gods that she hadn't hurt anyone else. After questioning witnesses and thoroughly investigating the lack of skid marks that had led up to the last few moments before her car flew off the road, they'd determined her accident to be an attempt at suicide. He knew differently. She must have passed out.

Hinting with his raised eyebrow and keen stare, the doctor obviously expected him to say something.

"Might her injuries be worse than you originally thought? After all, she shattered bones in her legs and her being submerged and lacking oxygen must have had some affects. There for a while, you'd wondered if she'd ever be able to walk again. Couldn't those dreadful shocks to her system be playing a part in her poor recovery?"

"Certainly, but as I explained at the time, once the swelling went down, those injuries were dealt with to our satisfaction. We've kept her sedated and as comfortable as possible. I must say, this lack of improvement is somewhat surprising."

Lucas reached out to run a gentle hand over her soft cheek. "I'll admit at the beginning, I was more worried about her face. But the contusions and bruising have healed surprisingly well after the reconstruction. They were the most visible of her wounds. You did tell me they were the least to worry about. Not that Vanessa would have agreed."

"No, I dare say you're right. A woman as beautiful as your wife wouldn't have settled for being marred by those horrendous scars." Dr. Hoven folded his hands together and puffed up like a bag of hot air. "Retaining the services of Dr. Weaver was quite a coup. Who would ever have suspected that the shy fellow I went to medical school with, would one day become a world-renowned plastic surgeon? Lucky for us, I knew him well enough that when I found out he was attending a convention in London, it was possible to contact him and request he undertake the operation."

"Yes, thank God for your having such connections. It was pure good luck. But considering my wife's grit and determination, I'm not really surprised she's fought this long." Both men gazed down at the blonde woman whose skin tone matched the color of the surrounding white sheets. Horrific blemishes, now mostly invisible, had faded more with each day that had passed. Her thick blonde hair, longer than usual, curled soft around her shoulders giving her an ethereal appearance.

Lucas drew in a huge, tension-easing breath and let it out ever so slowly. From under his eyelashes he watched the admiration the doctor couldn't hide. The tart was beautiful. He'd give her that. She reminded him of a Lily of the Valley, a tiny white, beautifully scented flower that was both gorgeous and poisonous all at the same time.

Dr. Hoven interrupted his musings with news destined to give Lucas another sleepless night. "There's one more doctor we'd like to call in to assess her. Since she slipped further into the coma, we've tried everything to resuscitate, without success. Dr. Robert Andrews is somewhat of a miracle man when it comes to bringing people back from the unconscious state. As our final course of action, he's agreed to stop by tomorrow and run a few tests. If he's convinced our findings are correct, then we'll make the necessary arrangements to take her off life-support."

Lucas covered his mouth, holding back his frustrated exclamation. Once he felt it safe, he replied, "Thank you,

Doctor. I appreciate your candor and all you've done for my Vanessa. I'll go along with whatever you feel is best."

"If Dr. Andrews sees no hope of recovery, no reason to let you believe anything can change, then I'm prepared to give you the next twenty-four hours in case you'd like to have your priest administer last rites. It would be a chance for the family members to say goodbye before we take the final step."

"I appreciate that, Dr. Hoven. My wife has no family left that I know of, but I will ask the vicar if he'd say a few words for her soul's journey."

The doctor nodded and quietly left the room.

Once the door closed, Lucas glanced all around the room and swallowed repeatedly. Emotions welled and threatened to overwhelm. Finally, relief settled the tumultuous flares in the pit of his stomach. It will be over soon. His fisted hand slowly unwound so he could flex his aching fingers.

For the last few weeks, he'd been ghosting the halls and her room pressuring the doctors for answers—for this answer. Now that his prayers would soon become reality, he could finally breathe. Lucas waited for two heartbeats to make sure no one else approached the door. Then he leaned in close to the lovely, empty face on the pillow.

"Soon you can say hello to the devil for me, darling. Because if there's any justice left in this world, you'll be heading straight for hell."

Chapter 2

Once she'd reached the hospital's spacious hall, Grace Joye wrapped her arms around her head, as if she could protect that which was already infected. She'd closed the doctor's office door, but she couldn't shut off the oncologist's words.

Three weeks! She could be dead within three weeks. Her brain was being destroyed by a... a growth. How could that happen? Pain hadn't foretold of the tumor growing in her head. Just a bit of dizziness which was getting worse and forced her to be sick more often. Symptoms she'd explained away as a flu bug. Until they'd gotten so bad she'd been obliged to seek care. The nausea and intermittent headaches had increased, but shouldn't there have been more of a warning? She knew things like this happened. After all, she was a nurse. But it wasn't supposed to happen to her.

She bit her lip to stop the building scream. It couldn't be. It just wasn't fair. When is it going to be my time, Lord? She'd asked that question all her life, and now it looked like he'd answered her in the most hideous way possible.

Being born with a large port-wine birthmark, marring her looks, had ensured Grace's childhood was fraught with nasty sneers from unlikeable children who seemed threatened by her face. Teachers and other parents shied away from looking her in the eye, and therefore she'd formed an early habit: don't discomfort anyone; cover up the mark, or keep the ugly side averted.

Though let down by her father, who she supposed had taken one look at his new baby's face and fled, her mother had loved her dearly. She'd been Grace's greatest fan. Her mantra—inner beauty always shines past what is visible and you, my lovely daughter, have an angel's light inside—repeated over and over helped Grace through the worst times. As long as her mum had lived, the days were bearable. But once Grace became a student nurse, she'd lost her precious ally to a heart attack. Nowadays, she considered Dr. Robert Andrews as her best friend, him and his housekeeper, Henrietta Dorn. He'd recently given her leave to use his nickname, Tobias, and she now thought of him in that way. Years ago at college, close friends had a habit of changing one's name to suit one's personality. Because of his good nature, his closest mate had dubbed him Tobias and the name had stuck. It was wonderful that he now accepted her in that way.

I'll go to them. The thought gave her solace. She felt the pain recede slightly and could breathe again. *They'll see me through this nightmare.* As of today, her position in this hospital had ended. According to Dr. Waterford, she'd be relieved of her duties, and he would deal with her official termination to make things easier for everyone.

Best of all, she'd be near Tobias, the only man she'd ever loved. A man who treated her as a woman he admired, and not a poor soul whose infliction made her different. Much older than her, he possessed the charisma to ignore her face and look into her soul, giving her a presence, a reality.

Hearing footsteps, Grace swiveled toward the closed door and tried to make herself as small as possible, hoping whoever had invaded her privacy would continue on their way.

Chapter 3

"Grace, my dear girl, what is it? You're pale and trembling."

"Tobias!" She turned toward him, looking like a lost child.

Trained to see people suffering trauma, the relief he heard in that exclamation couldn't be dismissed.

If it weren't Grace, he wouldn't have been quite so quick to interfere with another who had shown such an obvious need for privacy. But how could he walk past this lovely girl who seemed to be in crisis?

His favorite nurse instinctively turned to hide the fear he'd clearly seen, and by doing so, scared the stuffing out of him. The fact that she hovered in the hallway outside of the oncologist's treatment room, looking as if her life were coming to an end, couldn't be ignored.

His arms reached for her, slid around her slim body and hugged her to him. He sensed the waves of anguish radiating from her small person as she pushed herself close, her own arms snaking around his waist and clinging tightly. Fear started to build inside him. "Grace, you're frightening me. Can you tell me what's making you so upset?"

"I can't believe you're truly here, Tobias." She whispered the words in a voice full of tears. "I had tea with Henrietta a couple of days ago, and she didn't expect you to be home until tomorrow."

Mundane trivia brought up by her to ward off explanations. He was truly frightened now.

"I came back early for a consultation with Dr. Hoven." Tobias had been called in to examine a woman in a coma. She was slipping away, no matter what her doctors had tried to do for her. Unfortunately, after he'd investigated, he had only bad news for the distraught husband. The flicker of liberation he'd witnessed for seconds before the distressed man had bowed his head told its own story of a grief so overwhelming that the end could actually bring relief.

A sniffle caught his wandering attention. Awkwardly, he patted Grace's back. "My dear girl, stop dithering and tell me exactly what has happened."

Before she could speak, the nearest door opened. Dr. Waterford stepped out, nodded at Dr. Andrews as colleagues tend to do, and patted Grace's shoulder. "I'm glad you have someone to look after you, Nurse Joye. You shouldn't be alone after such a dreadful prognosis."

The man's chubby-face and bulbous eyes reeked with sadness. He nodded at Tobias, looked as if he would say something, but then shrugged and walked to the open elevator. The evident concern and the tightening around his lips revealed his distress. Before the elevator doors could close, he reached with his hands to stop them and said, "You might want to use my office for some privacy, Robert. I'll be at lunch for at least an hour."

"Appreciate that. Thanks, Frank."

Once Tobias had guided Grace back into the room and helped her into the chair she'd just vacated, he waited patiently. As a prominent psychiatrist, he'd witnessed many people shocked by bad news, and Grace showed all the symptoms of having received the worst. Giving her a few moments to recover somewhat, he passed her the clean handkerchief he was never without and sighed with relief when she accepted it. Always a good sign that patients hadn't receded so deeply into themselves that any offers of help would be refused.

Her voice, like that of a scared little girl, was raspy and so soft he had to lean closer to be able to hear the words. "I'm dying from an aggressive and deadly brain tumor, Tobias."

Oh no! He stuffed his hands in his pockets to hide his fists. "Dr. Waterford told you this just now?" He retained his professionalism, but only just.

She nodded and then used the hankie to wipe at her drenched cheeks. The paleness on the one side of her face enhancing the blemish's discoloration on the other, made the contrast sharp and much more defined. Her anguish being so intense, she'd forgotten to turn away or cover her birthmark.

"He just told me that I have a glioblastoma multiforme and it's untreatable." Her big eyes opened wide, amplifying her fear, and it cut him to the quick. A sob escaped, and she squelched it by pushing the cloth against her trembling lips.

The words 'inoperable tumor' bashed around in his head like a wild bird caged for the first time. A disgusting growth was flourishing inside this angel's beautiful skull, killing her.

"My God, Grace. I'm ever so sorry. My darling girl, what you must be feeling right now. Don't hold it back—not with me. Come here."

He knelt beside her as she slid out of the chair and nestled on the floor in his arms. He rocked her, patting her back—a comfort to them both. Words burst out before he thought to choke them off. "So much pain this morning. I had to deliver a death sentence for my first patient, and now this. It's unbearable."

While listening to him, her control broke and she wailed. "I've only just turned thirty. I never thought I would die so young. After all, I've never really lived. You know what it's like, Tobias, all those years of studying ridiculous hours to get my nursing degree and then going straight to work at the hospital." Tears streaming, she pushed away from him so she could look him in the eye. "I've never experienced having a boyfriend, or making love, or... What is it, Tobias. What are you thinking?"

The sly expression he wore couldn't be covered quickly enough. "Stop crying now, Grace. I think I may know of a way out of this predicament."

"I'm dying, Tobias." A giggle broke through, surprising them both. "I don't quite think of this as a predicament like running out of money or needing a place to live, do you?" A small but obvious smile curled upwards on the unblemished side of her face. Similar to a child, she swiped at her wet cheeks with the back of her hands.

As if leveled with a right hook, suddenly the perfect solution had struck. Like a computer, his mind flashed messages which were filtered and either accepted or deleted while the beginnings of a plan formed. With trembling hands, he lifted her with him as he stood. "I have a wonderful idea, Grace. There's no time to lose. We need to go to the house and coerce Mrs. Dorn into helping us. While we drive there, I'll work out the kinks and explain it to both of you at the same time. But first I must call the Vicar."

"The Vicar? Tobias, what are you up to? You're frightening me."

Tobias grabbed her face between his hands and planted a kiss smack dab on her lips. "Oh Grace, I've just figured out a way to save you and the beloved wife of a distraught fellow. No more now. You must let me think."

Chapter 4

Lucas waited for Dr. Andrews to leave before setting his emotions loose. He'd been given the news he'd prayed for: Dr. Andrews couldn't save his wife. The bitch was a goner and they'd be relieving him of this intolerable burden tomorrow.

If Vanessa had recovered, he accepted that he would have filed for a long-overdue divorce. It shocked him to realize he no longer wanted to kill her, although he would have that night if she hadn't driven her car into a ravine. While she shared this world, he'd have carried his hatred to mark his soul until the day he died. This way, with help from above, he believed in time he'd be able to forgive her despicable behavior.

He went to stand next to her bed, and like countless times before, he searched Vanessa's face for signs of wickedness. All he saw was a young woman, soft hair curling around a heart shaped face so lovely, a person had to look twice to be sure she wasn't an angel.

"Blasted hell!" He cursed at the memories as they overrode his ability to shut them off. Her ethereal appeal had been his downfall. Fact was, he'd fallen in love with the slender beauty at a friend's wedding in London before they'd even been introduced.

Vanessa Grey had been her name and he'd meant to change it to Vanessa Knight after his first sighting. Travelling from Bury to London, carrying on a romance had been difficult but exciting. She'd worked in a high-end gallery as a pampered artist who restored old works of art, and they'd spent many weekends touring other galleries and museums—a favorite pastime for Vanessa. With few friends and only her work to satisfy her, she'd made a life for herself in a small, well-kept, but rather impersonal apartment. The girl had worn lovely clothes and was immaculately turned out for every occasion, and he'd been a proud escort.

Though she'd played hard to get, he'd fought to win her over to marriage. Lucas supposed she'd loved him enough to finally give in to his constant begging and his romantic demands.

Close-mouthed about her earlier years, an introvert who carried it to extremes, she'd seemed content as his wife and with the good life his busy architectural business provided. She'd been able to move her work to a studio he'd built for her in their home and they'd been relatively happy the first few years, though cut off from others, which was her choice, not his.

Until she'd become pregnant.

Then the mad she-wolf had appeared. With the news she would be having a baby, she'd changed beyond anything he could have imagined, and it had taken him quite some time to accept the new Vanessa.

Unknown to him, she'd had her tubes tied. All the times he'd opened the discussion about them starting a family, she'd put him off and pretended to be as distraught as he was when each month nothing had happened. Therefore, when the unexpected had occurred, she'd gone berserk and his first glimpse of the real hellion had appeared.

She'd ranted at the doctors for their obvious ineptness as far as her operation had been concerned. Then she'd tried every way possible to get rid of 'it', her nickname for his baby.

When nothing had worked, she'd resorted to pleading with him to let her terminate the pregnancy. "We're happy, Lucas. A baby will only spoil everything. Please. I don't want to be a mother. I-I'm not built that way. It isn't possible."

Being a good guy, loving her and wanting her happiness, but needing his child, he'd cajoled her, insisting that it would all turn out fine—that they'd learn together and be good parents as long as they helped each other. Those heart-felt words hadn't made any dent at all in her wall of detachment.

Finally, he'd resorted to begging, all to no avail. She'd held fast to her demands and shut him out. How could she think of destroying the one thing he'd prayed for and looked forward to all his life—being a father?

He'd thanked God she'd been almost three months along by the time she'd gotten the news. Even then, she'd tried to abort his son, and only the fact that he'd watched her every step of the way, even going so far as having her followed, had stopped it from happening. For him, it had been the beginning of the end.

What kind of a woman would try and kill her own baby? His baby? Repeatedly, she fired at him, "A kid was never part of the deal." Still, he'd hoped that once she saw the infant, bonding would take place naturally and she'd change.

Not so.

Over the next few months, everything had gone to hell in a hand-basket. Always one to hide her true feelings, Vanessa became downright sneaky. Mean-spirited, she'd done everything she could to alienate anyone who cared. As far as he'd been concerned, the changes were unacceptable.

Always innately a happy sort of bloke, his good nature had fled, to be replaced with anger he couldn't seem to control. Anger against a wife who – by the very way she was behaving – was making his life into one big fat lie. Questions screamed in his head until, half-crazy, he'd visited his mother in London to beg for understanding of the female mind.

Though Vanessa had tried to be cordial with his mother, her coolness and unsavory attitude had forced the poor woman to stay away. But Lucas had had no doubt she'd help him now if she could. Therefore, he hadn't hesitated.

Both his parents had been wonderfully supportive to a young man who tended to get into scrapes like the rest of his mates. They'd stood by him, and he loved them dearly. Once his father had passed, he'd had good intentions of spending more time with his mother, but he hadn't considered his wife and her animosity. He wouldn't have blamed his mum if she'd wanted nothing to do with him and his problems, but the lady had come through like the gem she was, except her advice hadn't rung true. After all, she'd never heard the maliciousness screamed by the woman who he suspected was beginning to lose her mind.

Worried beyond reason, he'd broken down and stammered out the words that had needed to be said in order to explain the situation honestly. "Mum, Vanessa doesn't want the baby. In fact, I'd go as far as saying she hates being pregnant and has no intentions of being a mother to our child. I've never seen her so hateful and angry. There's a darkness in her that's destructive and... and downright mean."

"Darling, Vanessa's hormones could be the cause of these personality changes. I've seen it happen time after time. Be patient. Put up with her machinations until after the baby comes. Once she sees the child, she'll fall in love, and everything will be fine."

Not trusting in his mother's explanation or even the doctor's opinions, he'd hired a nanny who'd started the moment they came home from the hospital.

Good thing too, because from the day of Samuel's birth, Vanessa had stayed as far away from him as possible. The years had passed and she'd gotten worse instead of better, and so had her drinking. So much so, that their four-year-old son had filched her photograph from their bedroom so he would feel closer to his mum.

That's what had precipitated the final nightmare. Lucas had come home early as his housekeeper had called him to say she had the flu and couldn't look after Sam. Thank goodness he'd returned when he had. He'd come into the house the back way and heard the screaming and fear-filled cries all the way from the rear of the house.

Running to save his family from whatever horror had befallen them, he'd arrived in time to see his half-crazed bitch of a wife haul off and strike his baby boy across the face so hard he'd flown backward, hit the piano leg and rolled to the floor. A large red welt swelled his pudgy cheek, while tears flooded past the heartbreak in his eyes.

Vanessa kicked aside a chair, and grabbed his arm,

shaking the little body like a mad bulldog killing a rodent. "You little thief! Sneaking into my bedroom." She'd shoved him toward the door, her strength lifting him off the floor. Then she'd thrust him from her as if the sight of him filled her with disgust. Big blotchy red veins in her cheeks had stood out. And her maddened eyes, bulging from their sockets, had glared while she'd shrieked, "Get away from me! Go! NOW!"

Lucas's howl of rage interrupted her vicious screams. Her pointing finger switched from the trembling boy now huddled in a ball by the door and, instead, she'd leveled it at him. Her face crumbled at the same time as she'd swiped at the tears coursing down her cheeks. "See, you fool. I tried to warn you. Keep him away from me." Grabbing her purse from the piano, she'd fled out the balcony doors and, in seconds, he'd heard her tires peeling rubber down the driveway.

A wobbly voice had stopped him from following to rip her black heart out. "Mummy hates me, Daddy. I was a bad b-boy. She's very angry."

Protectively, he'd scooped the golden-haired boy up into his arms and rained kisses on his face, being careful not to press on the now-swollen cheek. "She doesn't hate you, Sam. She – she's just tired."

"I took her picture." The photo, still clutched in his tiny hand, now looked wrinkled and soiled.

"Yes, you did. Can I ask why you wanted it?"

"So-so I could say goodnight to her. She doesn't come to my room to say goodnight, Daddy. I wanted to..." Tears had clogged the little boy's voice at this point and the words had been lost between sobs.

"She didn't mean to hurt you, my boy. I promise you, she'll be very sorry when she returns." And Lucas had meant to see that promise carried out, except that she never did return. Instead, Inspector Goodwin had shown up at his front door with the news of his wife's accident.

***

A knock drew Lucas from the past. When he looked up, Vicar Witherby bustled into the room, his kindly eyes full of compassion.

"Lucas, my boy, I'm ever so sorry about Vanessa. I've been praying for her recovery, but it seems that won't be the case. Tomorrow, they'll be letting the poor lass find her peace with our Father."

Shocked, Lucas stuttered. "H-How did you know?"

"Dr. Andrews called me and said you were pretty distraught and might need my support. I rushed here as quickly as possible." He shuffled over to hold both Lucas's arms. Being a short little guy, it was easier to reach for Lucas's elbows. His small hands squeezed. Lucas supposed it was his way of commiserating and sharing grief. "I'm here for both you and Samuel. It's a terrible thing for a boy so young to lose his mother."

Lucas patted the clutching hands and then broke away. He knew the vicar believed him to be overcome; he just couldn't take the chance that this surprisingly wise old fellow would zero in on the truth.

The vicar had moved closer to the bed and was looking down at the vision of loveliness. Her face, now devoid of the bandages that had hidden the bruising and scars from the first few weeks, looked like a white marble mask.

The vicar's hand rose and his fingers gently caressed the pale cheek. "Poor frightened child. She was in such anguish. I'd hoped to help her, but she shut me out and suffered alone."

"Excuse me? What are you saying?"

"Your wife spent many hours kneeling in my church, praying and weeping. I begged her to let me help, but she politely thanked me and refused to talk. Most times she'd get up and leave. Finally, I stopped interrupting the peace she sought."

"I never knew."

"She's a sad little soul. Breaks my heart, it does. I wish she could have accepted my help."

"She wouldn't let anyone help. Trust me, I tried, Father."

"I know, my son. You're a good husband and a wonderful daddy. If there's any way the church can assist with your coming ordeal, please let me know. We are here for you and your family."

Chapter 5

"Don't squish her to death, Mrs. Dorn. Remember, she's suffering from a brain tumor. We'd like to keep her alive until we can save her life." Both women stared at Dr. Andrews with amused looks. "Confound it! I'm starting to sound like you. I obviously need a vacation." His sigh went on, followed by his head waggling back and forth. It made the two teary-eyed women smile, just as he'd intended.

"Shame on you, Doctor. At a time like this, how dare you make us laugh? Me heart's breaking over this horrible news, and you're making silly jokes."

"I know, my dear, but we need to remain calm if we're to have any chance to carry off my plan."

"Blimey! The plan. You want to use the magic of the vicarage roses, prick Grace and Vanessa Knight's fingers at the same time, so that Grace's essence will... ahh...shift into to the body of a dying woman, no less. God luv ya, sir, they'd stick us all in a padded cell if anyone could hear us talking about...what did you call it? Right! *Spirit replacement*. Them blokes that works in the mental wards, they'd be right happy to see the likes of us, I'd wager."

Mrs. Dorn looked at Grace and her boss, nodding sagely. The other two copied her motion in unison. "And... your point?" said Dr. Andrews, quirking one eyebrow.

The older woman comically dropped her forehead onto the surface of the table, banging it so hard the tea dishes rattled.

Taking sympathy on the old dear, Tobias continued. "Except that we know it can be done, don't we, Mrs. Dorn? We've had so many experiences; I'm beginning to feel like an authority on this phenomenon."

He thought back to the numerous hours he'd spent pouring over paranormal studies in every medical journal he could get his hands on, going as far as studying old myths and legends in order to learn what powers the strange plant possessed—even sending a portion of a branch to be tested in an American laboratory, but with no significant results. Other than becoming somewhat knowledgeable on the subject of comas and being constantly invited to give lectures on the topic at medical conventions, he'd found no concrete scientific evidence to explain how this enchanting rose plant, that grew three different colors of roses from one root, triggered the unbelievable switch.

He'd first come across the miracle in 1963, when a town librarian had been joined with a model from the future. It had taken both him and his colleague, Dr. John Norman, to come up with the unbelievable reasons as to why the event had occurred, and the knowledge of how to undo the spell. Since then, he'd had a few other adventures with the same rose bush. In fact, his sixteen-year-old niece had suffered a similar experience and, with the help of both Mrs. Dorn and Grace Joye, he'd managed to separate her from the body of the American reporter she'd fallen in love with.

Mrs. Dorn coughed and cut off his introspection. "Can't argue with the truth. You are the expert." Pride was obvious in her voice. "But I fancy anyone could argue that it's a-a magical substance from a blasted rose bush that's making this 'appen."

Both Grace and Dr. Andrews shrugged but said nothing.

"Cor, you're right, I suppose. There is no other explanation, is there?"

Finally, Grace pointed to where a pot of spindly branches with small green leaves, pink rose buds and hidden thorns sat on the side of the large wooden table where they'd taken tea. "I didn't know you'd propagated another rose plant, Tobias. What possessed you to do such a thing?"

"Actually, I started two new plants, one for my niece Dani to take back to Chicago with her, and because of the situation with Dani, where we were forced to steal her body from the hospital ward in the dead of night; I felt it prudent for us to have a transportable model of our own."

Pointing, Mrs. Dorn said, "You truly believe that tiny sprout you call a bush, with three puny pink roses will have the same effect as the magic one in your garden?" Mrs. Dorn scoffed like no one else. She'd snort and level a laser-like glare worthy of any highly-paid defense lawyer trying to intimidate a witness on the stand.

"I do believe so, my dear. I've never mentioned this, but John Norman and I have successfully tested it."

"Blimey, and I never knew. Hang on... I've been moving that silly thing all this time and could have pricked me finger by accident. Why didn't you tell me?" The woman grabbed at the sides of her head comically, her fingers getting caught in the curly mesh of a home perm gone wrong.

"Because you've been told to leave the gardening to me."

"As if you ever get around to it." Even mumbled, the other two heard the words clearly and looked away so the frustrated woman couldn't see their grins. No one cleaned like her ladyship, most of all the man she revered, but who couldn't be trusted when it came to dusting in her domain.

Grace broke into the fray before everyone lost sight of the issue, her beseeching expression mirroring her worry. "You're sure the experiment will work in this case? My spirit will travel into this poor woman's body?"

First Mrs. Dorn loudly cleared her throat, and then she spoke. "I hate to be a flaming naysayer, but need I remind you two, the specialists are expecting that the poor dearie will die tomorrow when they pull the plug."

"Mrs. Dorn!?" Grace's shocked giggle pleased Tobias. From the minute they'd arrived at his home, where she'd been enclosed in the chubby arms of his housekeeper, then forced to sit and drink the tea Mrs. Dorn felt was a panacea to any problem, her pale haunted expression had been replaced with acceptance and now a sign of her old pluckiness.

"Sorry, lass. But confound it! I don't know the other lady. God's honest truth, I can't bear the thought of never again taking tea with you. Think, pet, if Mrs. Knight hasn't any more use for her perfectly good body, then it seems reasonable for you to borrow it and live out the rest of your life. Don't it, Doctor?"

Normally the marring wart on the end of his housekeeper's nose faded, overtaken by her wonderful smile and the merry gleam in her eyes, but today was very different. Worry covered her demeanor like a shroud and the bulbous mark protruded.

"It's exactly what I believe, my good woman. I'm a doctor, sworn to save lives." He turned and stared at Grace. "Mrs. Knight's body has undergone huge trauma, as I'm sure you know, Grace. Anesthetized, she's dealt with a lot of pain. There were broken bones in her legs and in one of her arms, and her internal organs were damaged to some extent. After all the procedures she's undergone, and over time, the other physicians, including myself, feel that she's through the worst. The reason she's in a coma was because of the lack of oxygen and a slight swelling in her brain. But even that's receded. We'd hoped for a full recovery. Instead she's failing."

He caught the questioning look on Mrs. Dorn's face, thought for a few seconds and continued. "The best way I can describe it is like when you flip an electrical switch. By using the magic at our disposal, we get you, Grace, to re-open her conduits. My dear girl, how can I let you die when I know I have the ability to save you? Come ladies. Help me plan this caper now, as we have little time for debate. Even though the weather forecast is predicting a huge storm, it has to be done tonight. We must sneak this plant into Mrs. Knight's room so we can prick her finger and yours, Grace, and then be sure to it take it away in case anyone else accidentally scratches themselves. "

"What shall I do, Doctor?" Mrs. Dorn leaned forward, listening closely.

"You must come with us. I know there's a convenient hallway leading to the stairs two doors from where they have the patient. Once the changeover is successful and Grace is in the coma, we'll carry her body to that stairwell, and if you can stay and hold her until I come around with the car, I'll zip in and we can carry her down the stairs. Then I'll drive her to the ER to drop her off as an emergency and everything should be fine from then on."

"Count me in, sir. I can handle them instructions."

"I have no doubt, Mrs. Dorn," replied the doctor.

"But who will stay with Grace... I mean Mrs. Knight? She'll be alone, Grace, I mean Mrs. Kni... oh piffle, you knows what I mean."

"I doubt she'll awaken right away because of the drugs they've given to Mrs. Knight. In fact, I'm positive that once you slip into her body, Grace, you'll sleep like a babe."

"But how will we know she's in there?" Mrs. Dorn made a comical face once she heard her own words.

"She'll be in there, safe and sound, trust me." The doctor patted both ladies' hands then surreptitiously closed his eyes. *Please God!*

"And you think I can save her life, or should I say her body? This sounds monstrous, doesn't it?" Grace looked to the others, but they both shook their heads and reached for her hand.

"It's your only way out, Grace. Don't think about the aesthetics; just thank the good Lord for providing this opportunity. Think! If he didn't want us using this magic, he'd never have let us find it, now would he?"

"It's true, Gracie luv. You tell her, Doctor."

"In my estimation, I believe that the brain itself is healthy. It's simply resting in a state of psychosomatic blackout. Eventually, with you residing inside and willing to bring it back to life, you'll have full use of her body."

Grace interrupted. "I've never heard of such a thing. If you know what the problem is, why haven't you helped the poor woman?"

"There doesn't seem to be any way of reaching those

poor souls who get lost. Many have spent years in a coma, wilting away until they succumb to pneumonia or some other ailment that takes them. Others die quickly. The way this young woman is failing, it's likely to happen very soon."

"And you think by me invading her body and taking up residence, I can restart her brain to use as my own?"

"Isn't that exactly the way the magic has worked numerous other times?" He rose, and his hands formed fists on his hips, while his stance became intimidating.

"Yes, but all the other times both spirits lived inside the one person. If we do this, I will have stolen her body."

"What dribble!" Mrs. Dorn's ample form quivered with fury. "If it were the other way around, would you like to think another could live through you?"

Without a second's hesitation, Grace answered. "Why of course, Henrietta. I... Oh, you sneaky devil." She wiggled her finger in the smug housekeeper's direction.

"There's yer answer then, Lovie. Do unto others..."

"She's right, Grace. Now! No more quibbling. We must get ready."

Chapter 6

The night nurse, white uniform stiffly starched, caught up with Dr. Andrews as he sauntered toward the room near the end of the hallway. "Good evening, nurse. I'll not disturb your ward at this time of the evening, but I'm here to see Mrs. Knight. I've thought of one more analysis I can try on her brainwaves. I've decided to use this quiet hour in case it shows a negative reading. Don't want to raise false hopes, you understand."

As he spoke, Dr. Andrews waved a rather fancy voltmeter past her face. Then he quickly hid it behind his back, knowing that the type of medical equipment actually used wouldn't be recognizable to a floor nurse anyway.

Since there wasn't a portable tester for such an examination, on his way out of the house, he'd grabbed the gadget the electrician had left in his hallway while repairing the chandelier.

"I'd rather not build up Mr. Knight's hopes. We know the poor bloke's been through hell as it is."

The nurse's telling expression mirrored her agreement. "Truly, Doctor. This is the first time that poor man has left her bedside for weeks. We haven't been able to pry him away since she began to fail. I think he's been waiting for her to come back to him. Heartbreaking is what it is."

"I understand she has a small son also?"

"Yes, his name is Samuel. Earlier, Mr. Knight asked us to fix his wife's hair and make her look less infirm before he took a photograph; he explained it was for the little boy who missed his mummy." The nurse's voice cracked and sounded suspiciously tearful.

"Not to worry, my dear. Tomorrow will bring closure for everyone. Do us a favor then nurse. Give me some privacy for the next while so I can concentrate on these readings. I won't need your help. Nurse Joye, who works with me periodically, will be arriving shortly to assist."

"That'll be fine then, doctor. The ward is rather busy tonight. The lightning from the storm has caused power outages, and we've been run off our feet. But, if you need anything, ring the call bell."

"I will. Appreciate your kindness." Just then the elevator door opened and a dripping Mrs. Dorn and equally wet Nurse Joye hesitated before stepping forward. Seeing them, the nurse swelled to threatening proportions and approached stiffly.

"There you are Nurse Joye. Dr. Andrews is waiting for you." She held her hand up in front of Mrs. Dorn to stop her from moving forward. "I'm sorry, Madam. Visiting hours are well over. And, as the sign clearly shows, there are no plants allowed on this ward."

Dr. Andrews stepped up to intervene in the same moment Mrs. Dorn thrust the plant forward. His hand brushed against the branch closest, the one with a vicious thorn protruding. It penetrated deep and all four pairs of eyes watched as he instinctively pulled it free, and then like a child, moved to put his thumb in his mouth.

Oh no! Thinking quickly, Grace stopped trying to shield her face and grabbed his hand. "Oh, doctor, here, let me see. You've gone and pricked your finger." She turned to the younger girl and using the staff-nurse voice that every doctor was familiar with, she issued directions.

"Nurse, could you bring us a bandage for the doctor." Then she looked toward Mrs. Dorn and smiled. "I'm sorry. I meant to warn you in the elevator that visiting hours were over, but I wasn't too sure of which ward you were headed toward. You might want to return...ah...tomorrow." As she spoke, she angled her eyes over to the stairway door and then smiled when Mrs. Dorn nodded, then winked in agreement.

Grace knew they were in trouble by the worried expression the doctor couldn't hide. What in the world were they to do now? Since Tobias was pricked, wouldn't the magic be flowing through his body? How could they follow the normal routine as they'd planned? Mrs. Dorn's agitated voice cut in on her qualms.

"Sorry to be a nuisance. I'll be leaving then. No need for the elevator, I'll gladly take the stairs. Ta-ra." The older woman bustled over to the door, and using her ample hip, she pushed it to swing open and then disappeared.

The nurse's "tsk" showed her annoyance, before she added, "I'll just go to the desk and get the doctor a bandage for his wound, shall I? Shan't be a min..."

Dr. Andrews broke in. "No, don't bother. It seems to have stopped bleeding. I feel fine now. But I do appreciate your consideration." Catching on that she wasn't needed any longer, the blonde in the stiff uniform shrugged and disappeared around the bend, and the rubber heels on her shoes could be heard squelching on the linoleum.

As soon as they closed the door to Mrs. Knight's room behind them, Grace started to shake. "Oh, no, Tobias? Our plan will never work now that you've been stabbed. Will it?" Her voice rose, unthinkable in a woman whose services every staff physician demanded for their patients because of her calmness during emergencies.

"I'm thinking, Grace. Look, my love, don't unravel now when I need you. We must watch for Mrs. Dorn's return and sneak her past that starched harridan roaming the halls."

"Doctor!" Shock turned to giggles as Grace admonished the man she trusted more than any other. "Maybe it wasn't meant to be. My dear man, if I could be allowed to stay close to you and Mrs. Dorn during my last days, then, at least, those last days will be happy."

"My god, Grace, what are you saying?" Tobias swung in her direction, grabbed her fidgeting hands, and then turned her poor face toward his so he could look into her eyes. "You can't mean that. You have your whole life in front of you. As Vanessa Knight, you'll have a family to love, a child of your own."

"Not mine. Hers!" She pointed at the still figure swathed in white, unmoving on the hospital bed.

"She threw them away. Tried to commit suicide. The poor man hasn't left her side for weeks. Grace, give them a chance. With a heart such as yours, you'll learn to love them in time."

"What if I can't? What if their lives are too different for me to adjust to and I make a fool out of myself?"

"Like we discussed, you'll use the excuse of the accident for taking away your memory. It'll be difficult but not impossible. He seems like a nice chap, my dear, one who's responsible for a small child without a mummy. Think about it Grace. You can build a new life with these two sad people who need someone like you desperately."

Tobias knew just which strings to pull, she'd give him that.

The door swung open and Mrs. Dorn burst into the room. Her hat sat askew on her tight curls and the rouge on her cheeks made her pale skin look bizarre. But the twinkle in her eye caught their attention and belied her next words.

"Well, this is some pickle now, ain't it?"

Tobias reached for the unbalanced plant she was carelessly swinging around, and his gin-toting housekeeper moved to grab it at the same time. Thinking the plant was going to fall; she reached for the branch and squeaked with pain as another thorn pierced her skin.

"Confound it, Mrs. Dorn. Now you've gone and done it!" were the last words Dr. Andrews shouted before he slipped to the floor to lie as still as death.

Thankfully, Grace managed to catch the plant and save it from being demolished. Both ladies moaned in unison. But it was Mrs. Dorn whose face turned a puce color before she stumbled backwards onto the nearest object. The chair groaned audibly with her weight and tilted a bit to the side before it righted itself with a thud.

"Well this a fine howdoyado, now ain't it?" Mrs. Dorn's words broke through Grace's shock.

She felt the blood pulsing through her head and knew her heart-rate had doubled. "My goodness, Mrs. Dorn. This is a major catastrophe. How will we ever be able to get the doctor out of here without the nurse catching us?"

Mrs. Dorn giggled inanely and spoke, making no sense to Grace whatsoever.

"You silly twit of a woman. Whatever possessed you

to drink all that gin when you knew we'd be relying on your help tonight?" Not only were the words pure Tobias, but the tone of voice made it unanimous. The doctor now resided in his housekeeper's body, no doubt about it.

Grace leaned closer and the whiff of alcohol became stronger. "Oh, no! Mrs. Dorn, how could you?"

"It weren't much, just a tot to keep out the cold." The whining voice that answered could only be that of Mrs. Dorn.

"She's snookered." The words came from Mrs. Dorn's mouth but were pure Dr. Andrews.

Grace realized her plight and breathed a sigh of relief to know she could at least count on him. "Tobias, are you very uncomfortable on the floor? Might I get you a pillow?"

"Have you lost your mind? You have to get me out of this looney bin that Mrs. Dorn calls her mind. I'll be a raving lunatic within an hour."

More giggles broke from Mrs. Dorn as she slouched in the chair, her hat now covering one eye, her legs splayed open while her handbag hung from her limp, chubby arm. "You're a hoot, Tob-as." Words slurred from between her bubbling lips.

"I do believe the potion has affected her in a strange way." Grace worried her lip between her teeth and looked into the housekeeper's crossed eyes. "What should I do, Tobias? Will it be safe to administer another dose from the plant to undo the magic?"

"If you don't, I'll be bonkers by morning. Yes, of course, you must. Don't you see, Grace, this has to be the best thing that could have happened. We can now go ahead with our original plan, can't we?"

Grace carefully found a smaller branch with a thorn almost hidden and broke it off. She moved toward the body on the floor and when an agitated voiced yelped "No," she halted. "You must prick Mrs. Dorn first and myself second, so my spirit returns to my body."

She followed his advice, and within moments the doctor started to twitch and make small movements with his hands and legs. Meanwhile, Mrs. Dorn released a loud snore and her head flipped over to the side, mouth open and hat slipping completely over her face, with only the netting that had caught on a bobby pin keeping it from falling to the floor.

Grace rushed over to help Dr. Andrews to a sitting position. With shaky hands, he pushed his still-thick hair to the back of his head and leaned forward to rest his forehead on his bent knees.

"God's honest truth? That was one of the most alarming experiences I have ever encountered. That woman's flamin' daft! Good thing she can cook like an angel."

Grace laughed, relief apparent even to her, and without thought she threw her arms around her dear friend and clung to his strength. "That was a close call, I'm afraid."

"Around that woman, it's always a close call." Dr. Andrews glared at Mrs. Dorn, and Grace watched his glare turn to a lopsided grin the moment he spied the woman in question. He shrugged and shook his head in defeat.

Grace whispered. "You know you love her dearly. Your act isn't fooling me at all."

"Maybe, but loving her from this side is a far cry from being imprisoned inside." He shook his frame dramatically, and she laughed as he'd intended.

Slapping his hands together, the officious personality returned to take charge. "There's no time for these shenanigans, Grace. Are you ready to give your future a chance to happen?"

She turned her back to hide her fear. Then she moved to stand next to the bed and lifted the lifeless hand in hers.

Can I do this? Should I? Is it right to take over your body? Can I love your family as if they were mine? Questions flooded. Questions she'd purposely pushed away earlier when she'd agreed to this caper. But there was no time left. It was now or never, life or death.

Chapter 7

Grace slid into awareness, but slowly. At first, the voices surrounding her weren't distinct at all, just a drone of irritating noise. Then as she began to accustom herself to her new body, she focused, and everything became clearer. She heard the night nurse pass on her patient details to Dr. Hoven, the neurologist.

On impulse she tried to move, but it felt as if she was cemented into a cocoon of cotton-batten. How much longer would it take for her motor skills to kick in? She couldn't even blink her eyes. *Try again. Nothing!*

The night before flooded into her memory. She'd spirit-travelled into Vanessa Knight's body, only to find that the poor woman was racked with pain. It was as if an invisible torture devise was attached to her head, with the aim of squeezing it to smithereens. Nothing else could describe the overwhelming pressure Grace had fought so hard against. Could it be the medications they'd been giving Vanessa?

As Grace had nursed for the last ten years and considered herself very knowledgeable about the specific drugs listed on the patient's chart, she didn't think that any of the prescribed drugs created these symptoms. Unless, once consciousness was regained, the sufferer just didn't remember—like when a woman gave birth—the memory of the pain faded, to be replaced by the pleasure of holding the child.

Tobias had warned her what would happen once they'd begun the process for her spiritual teleportation. Months earlier, he'd enacted experiments with his colleague, Dr. Norman, and because of that, he could describe the procedure and what would follow.

Hers had differed in every way. He'd forgotten to mention the utter aloneness she'd experience, or the mental barriers she'd spent most of the night breaking down. Drained of all energy, exhausted and scared, she'd finally succumbed to the medications a nurse had injected earlier this morning.

Now, the neurologist was here, and the time had come to see whether their plan would work. Whether or not the magic from the rose could break through nature's will. After all, the woman whose body she now occupied had been declared brain-dead by all of the specialists. Even Dr. Andrews had determined that Vanessa would die once taken off life-support. Not because her body wasn't sound, but because her brain wasn't functioning to keep things working. Instead, machines were directing her life force.

Except that now Grace was the director and she felt a renewed life force flowing from inside, though she wasn't too sure if it was her own or that of the woman's body she'd invaded. This spirit-sharing was like nothing else she'd ever experienced. Strange wouldn't even come close to describing the sensations but she knew of no other word—strange, but surprisingly instinctive.

Sounds of a door opening broke into her musings and then she heard Dr. Hoven speak. "I didn't expect to see you here this morning, Doctor."

Tobias answered in his appealing way. "I felt obligated to attend and show my support for Mr. Knight during this difficult time." Grace felt her hand being raised and a firm pressure as it was squeezed. No wonder she loved the dear man. He'd never leave her to go through this crisis alone. He was ever so considerate.

Dr. Hoven's next words were surprising and uplifted her somewhat. "Earlier, these machines were picking up a peculiar reading for a short spell. Therefore, the nurses gave Mrs. Knight a small dose of medication. Not sure what caused the fluctuations, but they've since disappeared. Probably due to the violent storm we had last night. We've ascertained that the power stoppage and subsequent generators kicking in were most likely responsible. When Nurse Shelby did her rounds soon after, the patient's stability had been restored."

Grace instantly became aware of the surrounding life-giving hum. It mesmerized and terrified her all at the same time. What would happen when the sound was no longer there...when they turned off the machines?

"It was the mother of all storms, I agree." Cutting into her thoughts, Tobias bellowed, the sound different than his usual low tones.

"I'm standing right here, Doctor, must you yell?" Grace pictured Hoven's prune-like face pulled downwards in his usual scowl.

"Oh, sorry. Seems to be a problem with my ears this morning." She heard clothes rustle and wondered if he'd actually hit at that appendage. Picturing him doing so made her spirit smile.

"Yes, well, moving along. My plan is that once Mr. Knight arrives, we will accord him some privacy to say his final good-byes, and then we must get on with it. No sense in dragging out the moment."

Again, the door opened and Grace felt the tension in the room explode with the new caller.

"There you are Mr. Knight." Dr. Hoven's voice assumed a jolliness missing earlier. "I've given instructions for you to be left alone with your wife to say your final good-byes before we proceed. Take all the time you need. We'll step out into the hall until you're ready."

Well! Grace figuratively shook her head. Didn't the silly man realize the pressure his words had added to the poor man's amount of permitted time? *Step into the hall!* If she could, she'd be shaking her head.

Grace heard the commotion of people walking from the room and then sensed someone approaching the bed. *I hope he isn't going to be too emotional,* she thought. *I couldn't stand to hear the man weep for the wife he's about to lose. Especially, knowing I've taken up residence in her body and intend to steal it for my own.*

A male voice began speaking, the tone hard instead of sorrowful, mean instead of grief-stricken—harsh with loathing. "I've waited for this day, Vanessa. Hoped I'd be here when they set you free for your final journey, straight to hell. Exactly where you've made me live for the last three years. Good-bye, darling. I'm glad I will never have to see you again."

Wha – at!!? Grace panicked. Her brain screamed. *No! This is all wrong. Oh, what have I done? This must stop. I've changed my mind.*

Footsteps were walking toward the door and the click as it opened exploded her nerves into shrapnel. This time when the same male spoke, he did so with composure and remorse that rang with false sincerity.

"Please come in, gentlemen. I find that I have very little left to say except for good-bye. Let's just get on with it."

Hostility such as Mr. Knight felt couldn't be totally eradicated in a few seconds. Grace prayed that the experiment would fail. How could she replace a wife he hated?

"One moment please, Dr. Hoven." Worry sounded in Tobias's voice. "See here, Mr. Knight. Are you quite sure this is what you want to do? Miracles have been known to take place all the time. We could wait another day or two."

"No!" Shocked annoyance rang out from the bereaved husband. "I couldn't go through this again. We must do it today... so my son and I can move on with our lives. Dr. Hoven, all the funeral arrangements are set. Please, I can't take much more." This time honesty rang clear.

The neurologist demanded, "Dr. Andrews, move back from my patient, please. We must stop torturing this man."

Grace felt her hand being replaced on the sheet and heard the hesitation in Tobias's voice. "I rather think we should give it more time..."

"Too late," said Dr. Hoven. "I've stopped the machines. Mr. Knight, she'll take her last breath presently and it will all be over."

Complete silence surrounded her—terrified her. She sensed someone leaning over her body and the wonderful spicy odor of Dr. Andrew's favorite aftershave wafted past her nostrils. Olfactory action streamed directly to her brain and triggered an emotional response.

"Goodness me. I do believe Mrs. Knight moved, Doctor." The nurse's voice rose in shock.

"Ridiculous! The woman's been in a coma and hasn't

stirred in weeks. Don't talk nonsense."

Grace's eyes popped open just as Mr. Knight pushed his way past Tobias to glare down at her. *My goodness, he's a handsome man*, was the first thought that popped into her head. The second was that he was the most traumatized person she could ever remember seeing. Shock warred with anger, and then a tiny glimpse of relief shone through for a few seconds. It was his relief that gave her the stamina to smile.

And it was the smile that triggered the returning anger. His sound of anguish echoed in the room where, otherwise, one would have heard a hummingbird's wings flutter. Then she watched as he pushed past the others to get to the door, wrenched it open and staggered from the room. Exhausted by her efforts, Grace sunk back to the serenity of her darkness. The last thing she remembered was Tobias leaning over her and whispering. "Not to worry, my dear, I'm here."

Chapter 8

Lucas headed straight to the bar opposite the hospital. He banged on the counter and ordered: "I'll have a brandy. Bring me the bottle."

In a voice full of compassion, the barman spoke. "Gov, looks like you have summat to talk about. I've got me listening ears on today if'n yer needin' to share."

As if someone else controlled his tongue, Lucas spoke. "My wife was supposed to die today."

"Supposed to?" The old guy scratched his head and the theatrical movement caught Lucas' attention. "Not sure I understand, mate."

"The doctors were going to unplug her life-support machine..." When Marcus noticed the confusion the bartender couldn't hide, he elaborated. "After her accident, they were optimistic for a full recovery. But as time has passed, there's been no improvement. The neurologist told me her brain functions have deteriorated. You see, they hooked her up to equipment that supposedly kept her alive. Only they couldn't leave her on it when they considered her legally dead."

The bartender, his thick head moving up and down slowly, took his time processing the information before it seemed to make any sense. "Right! Now I've got ya. It's a machine what's keeping her alive."

"Not anymore. They shut it off." Lucas looked over the shoulder of the confused barman in front of him and saw his reflection in the mirror. Swollen eyes stared back from a face that looked positively horrified. He squeezed them shut to block out his image. Where had the friendly, happy-go-lucky lad from his youth gone?

The wheezy voice of a two-pack-a-day smoker broke into his musings. "You've lost me, mate. Didn't you say they cut off her life support?"

"They did! Only she didn't die. She's alive. And the bitch smiled at me."

Lucas had thrown back the first drink in one gulp and then poured another. Down it went in a continuous arm motion—*pour brandy, drink brandy, slam glass on the counter, fill again.*

A large hand stilled his movement, forcing his own to stay on the table.   Stymied, Lucas stared into the wise old eyes, read the sympathy and dropped his head wearily. He rubbed at his tired face muscles and groaned. "I'm sorry. You must think I'm insane."

"Not a'tall. You've had a bad day. Do us a favor then. Tell me your name? You look kinda familiar, for some reason."

"Lucas Knight. If I recall correctly, my wife Vanessa was one of your regulars." Sarcasm pulsated.

"Mrs. Knight. Of course, I remember the lady—"

"Lady?" Lucas snorted. "She was no lady, she was my wife!" The silly cliché made him chuckle, until a sob broke through which then made him squeeze his lips together.

The old guy bristled instantly. "You don't know yer arse from yer elbow. Mrs. Knight was one of my favorite customers. Never put up with any nonsense from the fellows, but had an open ear for anyone in real trouble. Even pitched in to help behind the bar a few times. Wouldn't ever take any wages."

Probably drank them! Lucas couldn't stop the thought from popping into his head, or himself from trying to visualize the person being discussed here. Was she the same woman who'd stumbled into the house most nights, then fallen into her bed fully clothed so that he'd had to wake her in the morning before the housekeeper arrived?

"My wife was—is—a lush, a cheat and a liar." Anger built again quickly. Needing to hit something or someone, Lucas kicked at the stool next to his and winced as it crashed to the floor. Ashamed at his outburst, he bent and replaced it slowly, taking the time he needed to cool down.

"Rubbish! The woman never left here drunk. Sad, sure! Crying, yes! But she seldom had more'n a coupla drinks. Most nights she'd sit here and moon over your photo, or the one of yer kid. It's how I recognized ya!"

Furious that this bloody sod had the unmitigated gall to argue with him, Lucas felt the last reins on his temper burst free. He roared, "My wife not only hated me, the spiteful tart hated her own son. The day of the accident, I came home in time to find her beating the lad and knocking him almost unconscious. I thought she'd killed him." The last words were whispered in a pain-filled voice. The horrible vision brought back the same sickening fury he'd felt when he'd walked in unexpectedly that afternoon.

His gut tightened, and he had to swallow repeatedly to hold back the bile that threatened to escape. "I don't know how many times before that she raised her hand to him. He never said anything. Just kept trying to be a good little boy so she'd like him."

Eyes, wide with disbelief, the older fellow broke in. "'Ere now. What happened to put her over the edge?"

"She caught him pinching a picture of her to keep in his room. The witch hit him over a flaming photograph. Want to hear something pathetic?"

The barkeeper nodded—his sympathy obvious and warring with his earlier skepticism.

"He took it so he could tell her goodnight before he went to sleep. He... never mind." Exhausted, Lucas felt empty, emotionless.

"Hang on 'ere. It's like we're talking about two different women. The person I knew loved her son more than anything else in the world. She told me so herself, she did. More'n once. God love ya, sir, you seem a decent enough bloke, and I'm sorry for yer grief. But if'n ya ask me, there's summat wrong 'ere. Look, I'm glad she's survived. You tell her for me, she's welcome back anytime. Now I think it's best that you go on home and figure out what happens next. After all, she is yer wife and the poor dearie needs yer help right now."

Lucas ground his teeth together, a habit he'd recently acquired. His choices were limited, and he felt like what, he imagined, a convict must feel after breaking out of prison. Then just when he believed he'd escaped, he was recaptured.

The old sod did have one thing right. Vanessa had nowhere else to turn. No family and certainly no friends that he knew of, other than the chap standing in front of him, looking worried. Therefore, because she was his wife—and that wouldn't be for much longer—he'd step up and take responsibility as always. He'd bring her home from the hospital until he could get his lawyer to start the proceedings for their divorce. Once she could survive on her own, he'd hand her the papers and wave goodbye... and good riddance.

Chapter 9

Since Grace's lack of strength only allowed her small movements, Dr. Andrews mopped her face up once again. "Do stop crying, my dear. I'm sure you were mistaken in what you thought you heard. Knight loves his wife enough to have spent many hours with her since the accident. Even the nurses have been impressed with his attentiveness. Why, the bloke's brought flowers, read to her, sat by her side. Nothing has been too good for her. Does that seem to you to be a man who hates his wife?"

In a melodic voice very different from her own shy sound, Grace answered, "The night nurses did tell me that he was ever so nice and even brought them candy." The whispery softness sounded strange to her, but not as feeble as the day before—the day when her mock husband had run from the room in a full-blown panic and rage that had left her shaken to the core. "It could have been the stress, couldn't it?" God, she hoped so. The unadulterated anger in his eyes had frightened her more than she'd ever been frightened before. How could she deal with a man so full of fury? Especially since she had no idea what Vanessa had done to fuel it in the first place?

Dr. Andrews answered, candor coloring his words. "Without a doubt! Shock can drive a person to act completely opposite to their normal behavior. Don't forget, the poor man had steeled himself to watch his wife die. The miracle of your being alive, Grace, must be overwhelming to say the least."

"You must call me Vanessa. Remember we discussed that I have to think of myself as her. Get used to hearing people call me by her name and accept that I'll be living her life." She sighed and continued. "I'm beginning to get used to her shape, which is so different than mine. See, her hands are long and slender and mine were so small." As she spoke, using all her concentration, she slowly lifted one hand in front of her face and held it there for a few seconds, before it collapsed back on the bed beside her.

"Why, Gr—Vanessa, that's a wonderful improvement. You're already beginning to get back your motor skills. But you mustn't rush things. Let the physical therapists work with you. They'll have you up and about soon enough. Is the pain still as appalling as it was last evening?"

"It's not as extreme. The cramping and tingling are slightly more tolerable. Taking the sleeping pill helped relax me and I was able to sleep."

"Rest will be your greatest remedy. This body hasn't been active for quite some time. You need to be patient. Maybe Lucas can help you build your strength by getting you outside in a wheelchair; take you for walks in the sunshine. It would do you a world of good—get some color in your face."

"Do you think he'll come today? I'm terrified that he will but hopeful, all at the same time. I'd rather have some idea of what I need to face than lie here wondering and worrying."

"Quite right, my dear. I have no doubt he'll appear soon and be ecstatic at your recovery." Dr. Andrews scooped her hand in his and kissed the fingers before wrapping them tightly around his own.

"I do hope so, Tobias. If not, I don't know what will happen to me. I'll have none of her memories or her small eccentricities. And because it's my power operating her brain, I shall inevitably draw from my own experiences and knowledge. Everything will be me, Grace Joye. Oh, Tobias, what have we done? I'm not sure I can carry on with this lark." Exhausted from talking for so long, Grace lay back on the pillow, her face colorless. By the end of her feeble remarks, Dr. Andrews had had to lean very close in order to hear her words.

His first realization that there was another in the room came from the look of dread on Grace's face.

"Not even out of the hospital yet, Vanessa, and up to your old tricks again, are you?" The sneer in Lucas's voice couldn't be ignored or misunderstood. Grace held her breath. Dr. Andrews was a very accomplished psychiatrist, and no one talked in front of him in such a manner without there being repercussions.

"I'll thank you to keep a civil tongue, young man. Your poor wife is suffering a tremendous amount of pain and cannot speak loudly. In order to be able to hear her words, one must lean closer."

Chastised and showing it, Lucas drifted closer and gripped Dr. Andrews's upper arm. "I'm most terribly sorry, sir. It's the strain making me behave so badly. Please forgive my terrible manners."

"It isn't me who needs your forgiveness, but Vanessa." Both men turned simultaneously to look at her, and no amount of will power could have stopped her blush. Her hand automatically rose to the left side of her face, and she wondered if her mouth actually dropped open when all she touched was smooth skin.

"He's quite right, Vanessa. I do apologize for behaving so abominably both yesterday and a few moments ago. As you know, our issues still exist, but I suggest we put them aside while you recuperate. Now, is there anything at all that you need?" At first, the man's voice was clipped and unfeeling, but by the end of his speech, warmth had entered and he once again became the person all the nurses raved on about; the one Dr. Andrews had first met—the gentle man.

It was the kindness that was her undoing. Tears seeped out and so did the first sob. "I'm sorry, Tobias. I don't think—"

"Who is Tobias?" Lucas looked around.

"Gr—Mrs. Knight. Don't carry on so. Take time and think before anything gets decided." Dr. Andrews grasped her hand once again and pumped it up and down in a very convincing way. "Think!" he repeated.

"Dr. Andrews, who is Tobias," Lucas questioned again.

"I am."

"I thought your name was Robert."

"Tobias is more like a family name. When I introduced myself, it slipped out."

"Well how did my wife know this?"

"I've been here all morning. I didn't want this poor lady to be left alone when she needed to be supported. After all, it can be terrifying for someone who has been locked in darkness for so long and cannot remember anything of her past. In fact, she doesn't remember you or her son, or anything about her previous life."

While he spun out the lies, obviously making them up as he went along, Tobias again squeezed Grace's hand in warning. In her mind, she decided it was a brilliant strategy. Of course she could have had some brain damage through having been in an accident and then in a coma for so long.

She glanced up in time to see the frustration that had appeared on Lucas's face being quickly replaced with curiosity. "You mean she has no recollection of her past? None at all?"

"I do believe that's what I mean. We've only talked a little, but from what I've gleaned; her only memory is of a person called Grace. Isn't that correct, my dear?" Dr. Andrews turned so only she could see his wink.

Lucas had approached the bed to stare down at her searchingly. His grey eyes warmed slightly as he saw the confusion she couldn't hide. A touch of huskiness in a voice that could rip or caress, he probed. "Do you remember me or Sam?"

To still her wobbling lips, she bit down and shook her head back and forth. If her eyes were as wide as they felt, she must look like a child caught in a lie. Hopefully the wetness covered up the fakery.

They must have. He took a deep breath, flexed his shoulders and awkwardly patted her hand. "Not to worry, Vanessa. Maybe we can coax Dr. Andrews to take you on as his patient. With his help, your memory could possibly return."

"I'd be delighted." Tobias spoke with satisfaction ringing through the words. "A beautiful woman such as your wife will be sorely missed by her friends, so we must work hard to see that she gets back her life."

As if Dr. Andrews's words touched a spark, Lucas

shrugged and tore his gaze from her face. "She had no friends, except for the bartender in the pub across the lane."

A whimper tore from between her lips. Before she could speak, a nurse opened the door and handed Lucas a large hand mirror. "I promised this to your wife earlier, but the wards were hectic, and I forgot until now. She wanted to see what she looked like."

Dr. Andrews's expression held shock. After all, he was fully aware that Grace knew what the woman looked like. What he hadn't realized was that it would be different for her now seeing it as her face—a flawless one.

Grace frowned and stuttered. "The nurse insisted I'd want to see for myse—"

Suddenly, Lucas leaned over her to hold the mirror in place. "Your loveliness is as always—stunning. Just remember the old adage, beauty is only skin deep." She couldn't look away from him. Handsome as sin, this man intimidated, and her nerves felt raw.

Powered by an inner force, his eyes drew hers. Attractive, pools of lighter blues were highlighted by darker azure sparkles and full of emotions she didn't understand. They held hers captive. As if by its own accord, his hand rose to wipe at the tear tracks on her cheeks. His touch was gentle, in direct opposition to the determination in his eyes. They narrowed, and his searching stare mesmerized until she purposely closed hers. When she felt him shake the mirror to gain her attention, she reopened them and felt all the blood drain as if sucked out by a vampire.

Then she looked into the glass at the beauty staring back. A swell of happiness burst over her as she watched a blush of pride stain her skin to a glowing pink.

Lucas groaned. His harshly whispered words broke her bubble. "You haven't changed."

Chapter 10

Lucas sat beside his sleeping wife and mentally tallied all the differences he'd noticed earlier. First, there seemed to be a strange attachment between her and Dr. Andrews, who he knew she'd never met before being hospitalized. He couldn't fathom what this cold-hearted woman saw in the distinguished gentleman, other than his obvious intellect. Looking at it from Dr. Andrew's point of view, Vanessa's charm could lure any man.

When he'd arrived to see the kind psychiatrist bending over her so solicitously, he had to admit to a momentary sensation of possessiveness he hadn't experienced in a very long while.

Another strange thing! Never before had he noticed such softness in her behavior. And her reaching out for physical contact—that she'd gripped the doctor's hand had staggered him.

Throughout their marriage, he'd always been the initiator of any touching, except in their bed after the lights were extinguished. It was there she'd let down her barriers and reached for him. Then, in a frantic sort of way, she'd made sweet love to his body and he'd accepted it as her way of expressing her feelings, showing her affection.

Those moments of intimacy when they'd connected had been some of the best in the early years, and he'd been satisfied, even happy with his marriage. Although they'd never had a lot of friends—her shyness, or so he'd believed at the time, had made her uncomfortable among others—she'd kept him occupied every night and contentment ruled until she'd gotten pregnant.

Now he studied the same woman while she slept the sleep of the innocent. He wondered how, over the years, things could have changed and become so dreadful? Like earlier when he'd stepped into the room. The look of confusion, even terror, she'd worn had made him feel like an ogre, something he could never have been accused of before he'd met her. In fact, he'd prided himself on being a likable, approachable sort of chap.

Of course, he'd changed. Not for the best and not in a way he liked. Honestly, over the last few months, he hadn't even been able to look at himself in the mirror. He'd felt like the lowest of the low: a terrible father who hadn't protected his child and the worst of husbands, one who'd barely been able to look at the woman who was his wife. What a flaming mess!

Clasping his hands together, his gaze landed on the mirror he'd held up earlier. The surprised pleasure that had lit up Vanessa's face still confounded him. It was as if she'd seen herself for the first time. He knew her to be a woman who took her beauty for granted, and to give the beastly woman her dues, she'd never seemed to pander to Nature's gifts.

He picked up the glass and held it until he came into focus. *You stupid fool. Don't get caught up in her trap again, man. Have a care. This is the woman who broke your heart, beat your child, and then tried to kill herself.* His musings made him flinch and the color ebbed from his face, as the import of those words caught and held. *Don't let yourself forget. No matter that she looks like an angel, she's a menace.*

The threat of seven years of bad luck stopped the temptation to throw the item he held against the wall as hard as he could. He rubbed at his temples and then searched for the aspirin holder he'd been carrying around in his pocket for months. Bloody hell! It was empty. He threw it into the wastebasket; the clang brought his head swiveling back to the sleeping woman who didn't so much as twitch. He slouched lower in the chair and leaned his head against the back. Tension oozed from his tight stomach and the muscles in his back screamed relief.

What was it about Vanessa that bothered him? Frustration simmered once again as he let his thoughts return to the earlier quandary. Dr. Andrews seemed competent enough, and a thoroughly nice chap. Perhaps a might possessive for his liking, and rather bossy also. Like when he'd forced Lucas to back off with that stern look full of unspoken warning: *Stop upsetting her!*

No matter how protective the doctor's stance, he hadn't been able to stop himself from reminding her, *as you know, our issues still exist, but I suggest we put them aside while you recuperate.* Those were the very words he'd spoken.

Puzzlement had been her answer. Her acting skills had never been good enough to fool him before, but this time, he could have sworn she didn't have a clue as to what he was referring to. Irritation had attacked, and if the doctor hadn't pulled him aside, reminding him of her amnesia, he'd have erupted.

All this clamoring anger needed to be excised, and each

day as he'd sat at her side envisioning what he would say when she woke had built the need. Once Dr. Hoven had admitted to not being able to cure Vanessa, that he'd be taking her off life-support, Lucas had tried to find peace. Searching in his heart for forgiveness, he'd wanted to bury his anger with her and had spoken to the vicar.

But it wasn't to be. She'd fooled him and lived. And found a protector. The short scold Dr. Andrews had forced on him, made Lucas aware that he mustn't upset Vanessa unnecessarily. With no other option, he'd treat her kindly for now, but she'd get her comeuppance before too long if he had anything to do with it.

Soft groans caught his attention. Her fingers twitched in a pathetic attempt to reach for someone. He could no more ignore her needs as squish a tiny kitten. After all, with her eyes closed and without that distasteful expression of contempt she normally wore, she could be the girl he'd first married. The one he'd fallen in love with.

Reaching over, he patted her hand and hesitated when her fingers groped and then clung. Slowly, he caressed the soft skin with his thumb and soothed her.

Once again, he decided that her fragile appearance lent her a softness that he'd never before witnessed. *I like it.* The instant the thought popped into his mind, he shut it down. Remembering her imploring look earlier, and how it had all but stopped his heart, he pulled his hand away. Could he be losing his mind?

She shifted her head in his direction, and without intending to, he leaned in closer. Soft curling hair fanned out over the pillow and framed her fragile features. He'd always loved her hair, pale strands of golden silk. Normally, she wore it rolled up and pinned in the back, very seldom letting it flow around her face. Until the nights when she'd allow him to use her brush and he'd immersed himself in the delightful shimmer of her thick waves. Hadn't happened too often, and certainly not since before her pregnancy.

While he perused her profile, he couldn't stop his feelings from exploding. *She's more beautiful today than I've ever seen her before.* Must be because her eyes are closed, and her usual glacial stare is hidden. *Give over, chump, stop thinking such rubbish!*

Lush eyelashes rose, and before he could sit back or look away, her gaze caught his. He hadn't noticed before how diamond-like emphasis made her usually dull green eyes sparkle. Nor had he been aware that the black irises were so deep; they could draw a man in until he lost himself. She smiled, and he snapped out of his trance. Those lips couldn't fool him. They were the same ones that had screamed hate at the person he loved more than anyone else in the world.

***

Grace held her breath to see if the soft-eyed man would return her smile, but the cold-hearted stranger replaced him within seconds.

"Hello!" The word came out as a whisper. She cleared her throat. "Have I been sleeping very long?" Searching the room, trepidation swept over her when she couldn't find Tobias.

"Yes, for some time. Remember, the doctor warned us that you need to rest in order to regain your full strength."

Hearing the raspy, deep mesmerizing tones, unlike many of the stern-voiced doctors she'd worked under, turned her insides to pudding. Grace relaxed and sighed when she didn't perceive any sign of his previous resentment.

"If you're searching for your Dr. Andrews, he had

patient appointments, but he said to tell you he'd be returning."

Now why did he have to spoil everything and become disagreeable? "Don't you like To—Dr. Andrews? He's a very fine doctor."

"Not sure how you'd know what kind of 'anything' he is, since you only met him yesterday, but I will admit to liking the man. He's approachable, not like that other idiot, Dr. Hoven, who is still recovering from the shock of making such a poor diagnosis in your case. Stupid bugger!"

Without knowing she would, Grace giggled. When she turned to face him fully, she became aware that her hand had automatically lifted to cover the left side of her face. She hesitated, stopped the movement and then answered the man perched at the edge of the chair next to her bed. "He did rather create a scene. Trying to blame the poor nurse, silly man! I don't believe he's worked here very long, and I have no doubt that he'll soon be asked to move on."

She watched the perplexed look sweep away the smile he'd shared with her. "Now how would you know that, Vanessa?"

Grace felt the red creep up from her chin and settle around her cheeks. "Ahhh...the nurse told me this morning. She's a chatty one and has many stories. It's all fascinating to me, and I like to listen."

"That's strange. You never would have before the accident. You'd have shut her off like a dripping tap and sent her running for the hills."

Grace faked nonchalance. "Would I? Bless my soul; I don't think I was a very nice person in my previous existence. I'll work to change those bad habits in my second time around, you can bet on it." She snuck a peek and watched his expression become even more confused. "Lucas, I'm most terribly sorry but I don't remember anything about our life or myself. There's a... a heaviness inside though, a weight that I think is unhappiness which seems to be ground into my very essence. It's disturbing and uncomfortable. I want to clear it away, and I will with your help. Just don't expect too much from me at the beginning."

Shocked, he leaned closer. "You've never spoken to me like this before... ever. I don't understand what's happening here. You look at me with those soft eyes and seem totally unlike yourself, and even though you're Vanessa, I'd stake my life on there being a difference so great there aren't words to... Bloody hell! I don't even know what I'm saying. Ignore me. Just keep being this woman and everything will work out. I'll help you through your convalescence, and then we'll find you a place to live."

"But I thought I could go home with you. I'd like to see our child."

The atmosphere changed instantly. "There's not a chance in hell you'll ever get near my son again." His chair crashed against the wall just as the door opened.

"Aye there, hang on, gov. You'd best be moving away from the lass, you ruddy bugger, or you'll be feeling my handbag upside yer noggin, so you will." Mrs. Dorn bustled over to the bedside and brushed against Lucas, forcing him to step back and make room. Even the netting on her perky feather hat seemed to bristle with indignation.

"My wife and I are having a conversation here." Lucas motioned toward the door. "If you don't mind."

"I couldn't give a rat's backside what you were doing,

but I know whatever you were saying has the lass in tears. I think you'd better give over and be gone 'afore I really get me dander up."

Shame flooded Lucas's face as he turned his gaze to imprison Grace's. Swimming in tears, she gulped back a threatening sob. Muttering an apology to both ladies—his tall body looking devastatingly handsome in a dark business suit—he strode purposefully from the room.

Grace arched toward Mrs. Dorn's waiting arms. The chubby housekeeper's allegiance had cleared away her sorrow, and a smile replaced the pain in her heart.

Chapter 11

"The man's a rotten bastard. I'll not have 'im near you."
An incensed Mrs. Dorn boggled the mind.

"Oh no, my dear. He's suffered terribly. I can see it in his
eyes. The poor man's a basket case... really. Think about
it. He was led to believe his wife would die peacefully
and probably had himself prepared. Only to find out that
she's... me. I'm alive."

"Then why isn't the daft bloke happy?" Having removed
her hat, the agitated plump lady plonked herself down in
the chair near the bed.

"Because I don't think he liked her very much. From the
little I've garnered from the few times we've been together,
she mustn't have been a good wife or mother."

"Rubbish! She...or rather, you, look like an angel. You
can't tell me a she-devil can be so beautiful on the outside
and rotten on the inside, now can yer?"

"On the contrary, Mrs. Dorn. I've seen it many times
in my practice," said Dr. Andrews, having stepped quietly
into the room without the other two noticing.

"Well, ye weren't here to see the way Mr. Knight went

for our Grace 'ere. Scared the Dickens outta me, he did."

"Mrs. Dorn, you must remember to call her Vanessa." Dr. Andrews turned to the woman on the bed. "What did you say, Gra—Vanessa?" He sighed when Mrs. Dorn snorted, and Grace giggled.

"He said he'll support me while I'm in the hospital, but when I was well enough to leave, he'd find me a place to live. Without thinking, I blurted out that I thought I'd be returning home with him–and that I want to see our son."

"That's all?" Dr. Andrews' shock rang clearly.

"Yes. My mention of the little one set him off. He seemed incensed at the thought of me being near the child."

The doctor put both hands in his pockets and rocked on his heels. "He told me something strange also. He said that the only friend his wife has is the barkeeper in the pub across from the hospital. I gather your physical landlady had a wee bit of a drinking problem."

"Oh, heavens, Tobias! No wonder he refuses to resume our marriage. I don't blame him for not wanting that kind of influence around his boy."

"Everyone has a story, my dear. And not all stories are as they seem. What say you, Mrs. Dorn? I think we have ourselves a mystery."

"I agree. Something's fishy. Look 'ere. I might have been a bit hasty in my judgment of the toff, I'll give yer that. But he's on my watch-list for certain."

Grace smiled at Tobias, his grimace not fooling her. He genuinely loved the old dear, as did she.

Without warning, pain began to radiate from her legs and the sensations made her cry out.

"The medications must be wearing off. I can actually move my feet just a little. My back has been aching all day, and I'm getting sensations of heaviness."

"That's wonderful, Grace. I'll have the nurse give you a rubdown and that'll help you get comfortable. Your recovery is proceeding perfectly, and we shall have you up and around in a matter of days."

"Should I be relieved or worried? On the one hand, I'd like nothing better than to begin living my new life and earning Lucas's trust and the love of our son. But without some kind of affection or, at the very least, hope, I couldn't be his wife. Maybe it will be for the best that we dissolve the marriage."

"Yes, you may be right. We'll take things one day at a time and see what happens."

Chapter 12

Mrs. Dorn plunked herself on a stool at the bar and waved her old friend over to take her order. "Freddie, can you brew me a wee pot of tea, and I'll be taking a nip of gin with it, if'n you don't mind."

"Why, good grief, it's Henrietta Dorn! Darlin', it's been far too long since your last visit. Mind yer, ya still owe me for the taxi fare to get you home that night."

"I sent it to ya in the mail. Don't you be telling porkies now." She pointed a chubby finger in his direction. "Ya did receive it, didn't you? Why, ya nasty teasing bugger?" Her worried look only lasted as long as the wink he shared.

"Come ta think on it, maybe I did."

Whiskers white and uneven, rheumy eyes shining with a decided twinkle, the older man leaned across the bar and gathered her soft pudgy hands in his large, dry palms. "Ever since you've been working for that doctor gent, I've missed you sorely."

"Go on with ya, you smooth talker. It's not me job that's kept me home nights but the rheumatism. After working all day, my body wants three things only: me rocking chair, the telly and a good tastin' cup-o-tea." She winked coquettishly, which made her mate laugh as she'd intended.

In her youth, Mrs. Dorn could have married this bruiser of a man who looked to be older than his years. But some of his baser habits had made her hesitate. His addiction to cigarettes she could have suffered, but it was his other two cravings that had repelled her: whiskey and women.

Not that it negated his charismatic personality and soft Irish heart. Those features had been his major attractions and still were.

Soon the requested hot drink sat perking in front of her and the pleasantries were taken care of. Now down to the real reason for her visit.

"I've been across the way to visit a lady-friend in the hospital and accidentally chose the wrong room. Vanessa Knight lay there, all alone, so I stopped to chat. She said she knew you."

Freddie stepped away from the bar, and cocky-like, angled his head. "Talk about telling porkies? That's one of the biggest I've ever heard, and coming outta those lovely lips makes me blush for ya."

Maybe it was that he used that word, but the color that flushed her face was a dead giveaway. "Now why would you go saying sumthin' like that, Freddie? Here I was thinking soft thoughts about the good times and you call me a liar."

"Because Vanessa Knight hated women. She liked the men fine enough. Not that she was a hussy, mind ya, but the ladies never got a pleasant look or a kind word from her in all the times she came into the bar."

"And that were often?"

"S'truth. She spent a fair amount of time here. Not that

she was a lush. Don't get me wrong. She was lonely—lonely and sad. She'd sit many a night and sip one or two drinks. When the fellows tried their luck, she'd let them down kind-like. If they was pushin' their luck, I've seen her take on the biggest lug and put him in his place without nary a worry for her safety."

Freddie scratched his mop of white hair and looked at Mrs. Dorn from under bushy brows. "Sorta reminds of another lassie I knew back in the day."

Now that made her smile. "You like her; I can hear it in your voice." Mrs. Dorn took a sip of her tea and smacked her lips loudly.

"I do. I've seen her lend a kind shoulder many a time to a sorry-looking bloke to cry on, but if a female approached, it was the cold shoulder they'd get." Freddie wiped the counter, his grey wet rag leaving a film that Henrietta itched to re-clean.

"For you to have noticed, it must have been quite obvious."

He pulled away from the bar where he'd been leaning up close and slapped his hands on his hips. "Are you hinting that I'm blind, woman?"

"Now why would I be so unkind? Mind ya, those two gents as come in a while back waiting for service might be getting a mite choked, ya think?" she said, with a defiant gloat.

"You cheeky devil. Never could see nuthin else when yer around, darlin'." Freddie swaggered over to take the order and was soon back, leaning against the bar in front of her.

"Now, where were we?"

"You were telling me that Mrs. Knight liked the laddies and disliked the ladies."

"Right you are. Many's the night I've seen her ignore overtures from some of my regulars. Got so's they'd leave her in peace. But it was strange, really. I've never known another who could turn so nasty from something trivial. I remember once, when it was really busy and Mrs. Knight put on an apron to help serve, and a harmless, friendly young lassie touched her shoulder just to get her attention. Without giving it a thought, Mrs. Knight slapped her hand away and turned mean as a cornered cat. She apologized afterwards for embarrassing my customer, but I'd seen it happen—and the look on her face. Cold as ice, it was. "

God love ya, Grace!! "The poor girl," Mrs. Dorn said, not realizing she spoke out loud.

"Not to worry, luv. Mrs. Knight apologized by buying her a drink and the incident was forgotten."

"I didn't mean her." Fear travelled from Mrs. Dorn's ample belly to her not-so ample brain. *Good grief, my poor friend. What have we done to you?*

Chapter 13

While sitting in bed, pillows supporting her back, Grace looked around her room with a new appreciation for comfort. She supposed she had Tobias to thank for her being transferred to this bright ward and out of the gloomy space where she'd spent the last few days. The polished wooden furniture that had replaced the bleak white furnishings in the other medical quarters gave an appearance of normality, making one wonder if it was still a hospital. And not being surrounded by ugly machines and tubes cheered her immensely.

Soft and pretty, with ruffles and bows she'd never normally wear, her gift of a silky pink nightie and housecoat dropped off that morning by a jovial Mrs. Dorn had brightened her day also. *I'm beginning to feel like a new person!* The inside joke made her laugh. Picking up her brush, she groomed her hair, loving the feel of the long thick strands curling over her hands, so different from her own thin hair.

The door opened, and the first things she saw were the vibrant pink roses framing a gorgeous plant being carried in by the young smiling nurse. Grace knew instantly who'd sent them.

"How lovely!" She'd finally begun to get accustomed to her new voice. As it strengthened, the tones had deepened. She'd overheard it said by the night nurse and orderly that she sounded sinfully sexy. Not that it was anything she could control, but it was disconcerting.

"I love roses. There's a kind of magic to them, don't you think?" The sweet young aide, nose buried, sniffed audibly and then moved to put them on the side table.

You have no idea. Grace laughed on the inside, and only a small sound emerged. "Yes. They're my favorite flower. Is there a card?" Not that she needed one. She knew who'd been so ingenious with the thoughtful gift. And after perusing the get-well message, it turned out she was right: Mrs. Dorn and Dr. Andrews had been sneaky by signing it, *Our best wishes always, Tobias and Henrietta.*

"Oh, this isn't all of your bounty today, m'lady," joked the blonde girl. "There's another gorgeous bouquet for you and it's from your husband, who by the way, is a dreamboat. All the nurses are mad about the man. He's ever so considerate. The dear chap brought a huge box of fancy chocolates for us to share in the nurses' station, and I've heard through the grapevine that he's made a grand donation for the new operating theatre."

While she talked, the flighty miss went back to her wheeled trolley and carried in a large glass vase brimful of stargazer lilies. The smell overwhelmed from the moment they entered the room, and Grace, not favoring this flower at all, asked for them to be placed on the ledge furthest from the bed.

A noise at the entrance caught her attention and she looked up to see her husband leaning against the wall, hands in the pockets of his flattering slacks while the casual black sweater, fitting and flattering on his lean body, turned his searching eyes into deep dark pools.

"You don't like the lilies? They were always your favorite," Lucas drawled.

"I appreciate your thoughtfulness, but I'm a bit allergic," Grace replied without thinking.

Dead silence filled the room and she felt a blush engulf her face, a deep giveaway that she was either lying now or had always done so before. The door closed softly behind the young nurse who'd scurried for freedom. Grace wished she could follow. *I won't talk,* she thought, swallowing with difficulty. *That way I won't get into any more trouble.* She lowered her hand from her face and clutched at her blanket.

Lucas straightened and wandered the room, stopping at the roses. "You have an admirer I don't know about?"

Phooey, she thought. Now what do I say? Deciding truth to be the better part of valor, she replied. "Dr. Andrews and his housekeeper sent them along to cheer me. They're wonderful, aren't they?"

"Hmmm." He nodded and then stepped alongside her bed, seeming to be nervous while also somewhat reticent.

Finally, she couldn't stand the tension another minute. "Is something wrong, Lucas?"

He stopped and sat in the nearby visitor's chair, surveying her from head to toe, his eyes like a laser as they travelled her length. Then he zeroed in on her face. She could have sworn the man's expressive smoky-blues were pleading and for some unknown reason a sickening rush of shame curdled her insides.

"Yes. I have to ask you a favor, and I honestly don't know what will work best, a bribe or a threat."

"My goodness. It sounds serious. Why use either? I'd be more than happy to grant you whatever you ask, be that it won't harm anyone."

He shook his head and sighed. "I don't get it. You're different. And I don't trust you. But your son needs you, and as much as I wish I could deal with this, you're the only person who can. Now I know you've never wanted anything to do with Samuel, but for once in your selfish life, I'm asking you to behave like a mother." The scorn he showered her with felt like shots of acid burning her soul.

His words slapped her soft heart and she felt battered enough to pass out. What did he mean? She didn't want anything to do with her own son? What kind of woman could possibly feel that way? Despite his glaring, she picked up on his desperation and her spirit snapped into place. The backbone vital to dealing with her particular life's challenges had kicked in with a vengeance. She clenched her teeth, swallowed, then spoke gently.

"Of course, I'll help. What is it he needs?"

"You must understand, Sam's very fragile right now and I won't have him upset. But he's also blaming himself for your accident and is making himself ill over it all. Between the lad's nightmares and loss of appetite, I feel scared and well... rather frantic. Last evening, he finally broke down and told me what's been making him so unhappy."

"Oh, the poor baby. What did he say?"

"Seems he feels responsible for your being in the hospital."

"Why in the world would he think that?"

"You don't remember?" His searching gaze probed her innocence and seemed satisfied when she shook her head. "Before you ran from the house, you'd been angry with him. In fact, you were furious." Again, his penetrating stare drilled into her as he leaned closer and watched her expressions. She knew he'd see confusion and empathy because those were the emotions that roiled inside.

"You really don't remember, do you, Vanessa?"

"No. Nothing. It's all blank."

Her answer seemed to satisfy Lucas, who stood tall and resumed his wandering. "He made me promise to bring him here to see you. Now, I want your promise that you'll be kind and tell him he's not to blame. Trust me. If there were any other way to settle this, to clear his little mind from the torture he's undergoing, I would do so in a flash. But it seems you're the only person who can help him."

"Of course I ca—"

Lucas, caught up in his speech, swiveled and leaned over her. "I've never begged you for anything, Vanessa. I've given you everything I thought would make you happy, but I'm begging you now. Please don't let our son grow up bearing this horrible burden. He's been so unhappy. I'll give you anything—"

"Stop! Lucas, stop. You're breaking my heart. I want to see the boy and of course I'll tell him it wasn't his fault. Of course, I will." Grace had reached out without knowing and had grasped Lucas's hand. With each assurance, she'd tightened her grip. Sincerity rang from her shaken voice to where even she could hear it. "Is he here?"

Seeming to be confused but hopeful, Lucas nodded, swallowed and turned away quickly. "Yes, outside." Did his voice wobble? She could have sworn it did and, if nothing else, that chink in his armor told her just how much the next few minutes would mean to him. She'd never let him down. Not only was he a thoughtful man, but obviously a wonderful father. Sadly, it seemed, he'd just chosen the wrong wife.

He left, and a few moments later the door opened again, and Grace pulled herself higher in the bed and tucked her loose hair behind her ears. One stroke of her now-smooth cheek settled her nerves and she smiled.

A small boy, dressed in short pants and a sweater, the spitting image of his mother, crept into the room as if afraid he'd wake her up. He stopped as soon as he passed the threshold, hesitating, waiting, fear imprinted on his little boy features. His hands were clasped in front and Grace could see how his fingers were pinching each other, twisting and rubbing. His father, looming behind him, placed a supporting hand on his thin shoulder.

"Hello, Mother."

"Samuel, I'm so glad you've come to see me. Please come closer." Grace motioned him over to her side. She smiled as gently as she could, and a coaxing wiggle from her fingers and encouraging nods drew him nearer.

"Daddy said you were better now. I wanted to see for myself."

"Can you see from all the way over there? If you'd like to sit up here with me, then I'll get to see you also."

First fear, and then a blossoming pleasure filled his little face. Green eyes, the twins of hers, lit up and a tiny smile emerged. "Daddy? Can I?"

"Sure, sport. If it's okay with your mother, it's fine with me. Can you climb up alone or do you need a lift?"

"A lift, please. I don't want to hurt Mother accidentally."

Grace spoke softly. "Oh, Sammy-son, you could never hurt me."

Lucas's head reared up at her words and his eyes narrowed. Sam lifted his arms. Both man and boy hesitated at her bedside, not sure what to do next.

"Come and sit right here." She patted the comforter

next to her. "Then I can hug you like I've wanted to do since you arrived."

"You want to hug me?"

"Ever so much. Do you mind?"

The youngster carefully leaned toward her and that was all the encouragement she needed. She gathered him to her, and as she soon as she felt his arms go around her neck, she heard the sobs that wracked his little body.

"Shh, baby, it's okay. Don't cry, my lad. Mummy's here." All the while she soothed him, she rocked his little body back and forth and placed kisses everywhere, his hair, his cheeks, on every surface covered with tears.

"Oh, Mother! I'm sorry I was such a bad boy. You were so an... angry with me that you got into an ac... accident. It was my fault, wasn't it? You weren't looking where you were going 'cause I made you lose your temper."

The sobs grew louder, and Grace became fearful that the little guy would never stop. Hiccups wrenched his body and the wails broke her heart into smithereens. Suddenly, she experienced a tremendous welling of emotion from within and it overpowered her to where she felt she'd lose consciousness. Afraid, staggering under the double onslaught, she reached her hand toward the man whose eyes were brimming over.

He came closer, gingerly sitting on the bed next to them and rubbed his large hand gently over the boy's back. It seemed to soothe Sam, and his cries quieted while he lay with his head nestled on her chest.

Lucas spoke softly. "Take it easy, Samuel. Don't cry so. Everything is okay now."

The boy refused to look up and burrowed even harder into Grace's embrace. "Sammy, please, you must stop, or you'll be sick. Listen, baby, the road was slippery, and I wasn't being careful. It was my fault the car went off the road, not yours. I didn't want to have to admit this but here's the truth: your mum's a rotten driver."

"You are?" Hope lit up globby eyes of green glass, and sniffles replaced the bawling from seconds earlier. His body relaxed, and he leaned away from her so he could stare into her face.

Grace had always had a soft spot for children, but since they tended to shy away from her birthmark, she'd never had the pleasure of any up-close relationships with them until they were sick and needed a nurse. Then she'd been in her element.

Having this precious little guy stare at her with such adoration brimming out of his gorgeous eyes filled her heart. Love, such as she'd never experienced, overflowed and oozed into every pore and cell until she belonged to him. From that moment on, she knew he'd be her first consideration in the same way that a dog knows its own pup.

She swallowed and prayed her voice wouldn't break. "I'm afraid so, Sammy-son. Actually, I'm really quite awful."

"Is that why you'd never take me anywhere with you?"

Sickened by the actions of the woman's body she now controlled, she shook off her anger and stared into his questioning, glistening eyes, then nodded. "Uh huh! I'd never want anything to happen to you, baby... ever!" She dropped a kiss on his soft blond hair. "But I promise you one thing. From now on I'll not go anywhere in a car until I've gotten lessons so I can learn how to drive better."

"Then you could take me with you."

She looked up at Lucas, a question blazing. His nod was hesitant but finally forthcoming.

She smiled at the boy. "I would like that very much."

The indecision the boy fought before he kissed her cheek was telling and, oh so sad. She leaned forward ever so slightly, encouragingly, and felt his warm lips caress the one area on her body that needed the tender touch. She knew before falling asleep, and every night afterward, she would relive that moment over and over again.

She hugged Sam once more, and like little boys do, he settled down beside her and curled up in her arms. With a loud sigh, his eyelids began to droop. Sifting her fingers through his blond curls worked the magic as he released one last quivering sound and then went limp.

Lucas shifted and drew her attention. Still pale from watching his son suffer, he rubbed at his cheeks one side and then the other, his hand finally covering his mouth as he leaned his chin onto it and stared at her with his head angled to the left.

Mesmerized, his grey eyes compelling, she couldn't look away, not even a little. His held her prisoner, and having no talent or skills in concealing her feelings, she knew her emotions were open to him like a picture on a television screen. *God, don't hurt me*, she worried, her skin flushing hot and cold—terrified.

Before she knew what he would do next, he leaned over and kissed the same cheek his son had moments earlier. When the little boys lips had touched her skin, love had resulted. When the man's lips touched the same place, she thought she'd swoon. Never in her life had a moment been so beautiful.

His hand reached up and caressed the opposite side of her face and he leaned forward to whisper in her ear. "We both know you're a terrific driver, Vanessa. Get better soon. I want you to come home."

Chapter 14

Lucas's words 'I want you to come home' echoed in her head, over and over for the next few days. That's what gave her the drive to push herself past limits of pain. As a nurse, she knew exactly what had occurred in her body—the broken limbs, the areas of stiffness and debilitation; how to work lax muscles and where to focus her energies. When exhaustion forced her to stop, her knowledge of the damage one could do being silly made her rest.

Knowing her chart intimately, she pestered the nurses to help her with frequent massages and heat therapy. And when the day came for her to get out of bed, she needled the therapists to work with her more than ever. Her crisp nurse's no-nonsense tone constantly came into play when they tried to slow her down. Eventually, she felt strength returning to her new body and each night she fell asleep exhausted but happy.

When she wasn't physically active, she would spend hours giggling with her daily visitor, Mrs. Dorn, who behaved more like a mama bear than ever. Protecting her seemed to be the role the older woman assumed, and

Lucas was her main target of distain. She didn't trust him with her lovely friend and told her as much. That was, until earlier that day.

Henrietta had been trying to teach her to knit. Hilarious antics commenced when Grace had somehow gotten the wool wrapped around her wrist as she tried to maneuver the long needles. Laughing so hard, the two were unaware that the ball had rolled off the bed and lay on the floor feet away. It was when Lucas presented it to Mrs. Dorn, as a long-ago knight might present a special token to his lady-love, that Grace saw the anger thaw in her old friend and be replaced with a growing admiration.

"Your royal highness, you dropped your golden fleece." He moved in front of Mrs. Dorn and his tall body bent from the waist as he held out the ball of fuzzy yellow wool. His eyes twinkled with fun, offering friendship.

As Grace watched the other woman melt under his gallantry and playfulness, her heart flip-flopped, and its rhythm doubled. She observed his delightful shenanigans to win over her best friend. Right then, she knew he would be as wonderful a playmate for his woman as he had proven to be for his son. Since it was the first time she'd ever seen this side of the man, she felt herself falling under his spell like chubby Mrs. Dorn.

Mrs. Dorn's countenance changed immediately. Simpering, loving Lucas's attention, she fell into the game immediately. "Why, thank you, kind sir." Flirtatiously, her eyelashes fluttered while her hands, pressed together, cradled one side of her face. "Grace..." A quick jab, and the quick-witted woman changed the words to, "My grace and I were passing the time in needlework. If you'd care to join us, kind sir, I should be happy to teach you the art of knitting also."

"I thank you, Mistress Dorn, but I do believe I'm already quite skilled. As a boy my grandmother used this as a mode of punishment when naughtiness overcame me."

"Oh, we'll need proof, sire," she said, as she handed him the needles and wool, a daring glint in her eye.

Without hesitation, Lucas took them in hand and started working diligently to knit and purl, obviously showing off his undeniable talent. He paused, winked at Grace who sat there giggling behind her hand, and then presented the bundle to a surprised Mrs. Dorn.

"Cor, ya must have been a rotten nipper," she said without thinking, which had them all in stitches.

The next half-hour passed quickly, and when an offer for a ride home was forthcoming and Mrs. Dorn bent to kiss Grace good-bye, she whispered in her ear that her husband was *loverly* and then strutted from the room with her new best friend's assistance.

Shortly after they left and Grace had once again worked at her exercises, she sat in her bed tired but happy. Each day saw her better able to walk and move freely, and closer to the date the hospital would discharge her. Going home to a waiting Sam was a priority, true, but just as high on her agenda was learning her place as Lucas's wife. Each day he left her with a chaste kiss on her cheek and shared memories as he told her about the life he thought she'd forgotten.

Only one thing had remained the same over this time. Whenever Grace tried to venture into her physical hostess's mind, she met with total blankness. Nothing! There were no faint memories or instinctive responses, at least nothing tangible. Those stirring responses during Sam's visit were finally explained by Grace accepting that it was her own emotions that had reacted to the boy and nothing else.

Just as she lay back to nap, Tobias arrived, looking very pale. The seriousness in his face warned Grace of bad news and she sat up again and straightened her shoulders in readiness to hear what he had to say.

"Tobias, something is wrong. Please tell me." Grace reached for his hands as he dropped into the chair closest to her hospital bed.

He cradled her palms in his and then closed them in a prayer-like position firmly. "You haven't asked about your own body, Grace, and I've been reluctant to say anything that would upset you, so I haven't mentioned your condition at all. But today I must."

"Is that why you've been staying away, Tobias? I've missed you and wondered. Henrietta says you're extremely busy, but I felt there was something more keeping you from visiting."

"I'm sorry, my dear. I have been busy, but you're right in thinking that I just didn't want to burden you with this on top of everything else."

"I'm dying, aren't I?" Her tone hardened as she swallowed repeatedly. "You can tell me the truth, Tobias."

"Yes, my dear. The brain tumor has increased in size and they can't relieve the pressure anymore. The doctors will be taking you off all the ventilators and they're positive you won't last the night."

A cry broke free as she buried her face in shaking hands. The waves of horror started in her mind but flowed throughout her body. Tightened stomach muscles, and painful spasms, made her all but pass out. Nausea built and, as her mouth filled, she prayed she wouldn't embarrass herself.

Dr. Andrews leaned closer and gathered her into his

arms. While she swallowed repeatedly, her face rested on his shoulder. He patted her back, then stroked her long hair away from her flushed face and murmured consolingly in her ear.

"I'm so sorry, darling girl. Shush—don't cry. It'll all be over soon. Don't be sad."

'It never seemed real, Tobias. I know I'm now accepted as Vanessa Knight, but it's crazy. Inside, I'm still me, Grace Anne Joye. Have I made a foolish mistake? I can't seem to think clearly." She pushed him back and glared at him. "You must tell me what to think, how to deal with this. I need your help, professionally, not just as my friend."

His expression hardened, a sight she'd never seen before. "There's still time to put you back into your own body, Grace, so you can die as patient Joye. Is that what you want? To give up Vanessa's body, ignore the son and husband who need you and leave behind two dead bodies?"

Shocked, Grace stared at the angry doctor. "Of course not!" Anger built inside her also, and her voice rose as she answered his impudence. "Sam would be devastated. He needs his mother. And Lucas needs a wife. How could you ask me those things?"

Dr. Andrews waited and watched, and she finally saw his ploy for exactly what it was. The way he'd intended it to be. She'd answered her own question. She'd chosen life—the happiness of a little boy and the love of a good man—over death.

"Do you want to be with Grace when she passes, Vanessa? If not, don't fear. I will stay by her side—throughout the night if need be." Grace knew by the way he referred to her with her new name; it was his way of reminding her of her future.

"Thank you, Tobias." She reached for his hand, hers trembling. "If you don't mind, I'd like to be there with you. After Grace passes on, I'll have reached the point of no return. I think once that happens, I'll truly take on this gift of the life you've given me. Maybe then I'll accept that I will forevermore be Vanessa."

"I'll fetch you later then. Rest now."

After the doctor left, she cried into her pillow until there were no tears left. Wracked with spasms of sadness, she looked back on her life as Grace Joye. Most of the time, she'd been a sad, lonely person. Her poor blemished face had put many difficulties in front of her and her future had always been gloomy. Not for the first time, Grace acknowledged just how fortunate she was to be given a second chance and, right then, she dedicated her future to being the best wife and mother alive.

Chapter 15

"Vanessa, you make me proud. All the nurses are extolling the efforts you're making to get your strength back."

Lucas sat on the side of the bed and watched as she slowly moved around the room, her filmy housecoat floating behind her like a silken shadow. There was a sadness in her spirit that he hadn't noticed before, traces of strain on her lovely unblemished complexion. Which was one of the things he'd always admired about the woman, even during the times he'd hated her. Her skin, pale and creamy, would please any model in the world of fashion and he knew for a fact it wasn't maintained with the help of makeup or chemicals. It was natural. To him, it had always seemed one of the strangest contradictions of nature, that the ruthless woman he'd hated had a face of such innocent beauty.

Recently, he'd begun to change. How could you detest someone who lit up whenever you entered the room? Someone who was kind and gentle to her visitors—who related to characters like Mrs. Dorn and her Dr. Andrews? And was always super-patient with her nurses? In fact, he'd even witnessed her teaching a young volunteer how to support a bedridden person to sit up properly. And she'd done it so gracefully that the girl had left the room with her head held high and a happy smile in place.

So how could a man dwell on the vicious wench from before that dreadful accident when she'd so obviously changed to the person he could love now, deeply, desperately?

Hold it! What was he thinking? Any romantic feelings he'd had for his wife had disappeared long ago. From the first moments when he'd witnessed her ruthless behavior after she'd discovered she was pregnant, her despicable conduct as a mother, and then the disgusting cruelty she'd heaped onto their new son, his previous admiration had waned to be replaced with cold bitterness. After her last contemptible act, hatred had seared deep. A need for retaliation had followed.

As these thoughts battled inside his head, Vanessa turned too quickly, missed catching hold of the nearest chair and, with a stifled groan, started to stumble. Instinct drove him to catch her before she hit the ground. They ended up entangled on the floor, him underneath her. He lay there with her resting on top of him, staring down into his eyes, and he watched as dismay fled and was replaced, first with shyness and then longing. Her hand rose to her cheek and then moved over his shoulder to the floor, so she could bolster herself away from his body.

He smiled, couldn't help himself. "I would venture to guess that you're not as strong as you thought? You have to give yourself more time, Vanessa." *My Lord, she's beautiful.* He took shallow breaths to control willful words that wanted to slip out. But he'd forgotten to place controls on his hands. They moved of their own accord and went straight to her face. Gently he lifted the golden mass of hair from where it had cascaded over her shoulders and, with hands full of silk; he cupped the back of her head while searching her eyes.

She sighed. The shaky moan penetrated his heart and built shivers that exploded everywhere. Most careened directly to his lower regions. The discomfort of being engorged for the first time in a long while made him swallow and then groan in unison.

Uncontrolled thoughts became words and escaped. "I can't wait until you're home, Vanessa. I need you desperately. It's been so long." He gently drew her face down to where his lips could reach hers and he kissed her.

Surprised and then shocked, he felt as if he were kissing a stranger. First her mouth refused entry, but she didn't pull away. In fact, she nestled closer. After nudging her lips to part for him, she opened little by little until he could taste fully. She was driving him mad. This side of the woman had never surfaced before and he found his rioting emotions close to going out of control. *It's like kissing a virgin.*

Her tongue finally met his searching one, igniting passion. Then she pulled back. Patiently he waited, stroking her, his lips softening and searching. His persistence paid off. Again, her tongue found his, this time licking daintily, seeming to offer submission.

It was the most erotic kiss he'd ever experienced, and his member swelled in full agreement. He wanted her—here, now.

"You taste so good. God, I need you, my darling girl." His hands shifted to her back and made their way to her sides, where he lifted her arms above them, so he could feel her body pressed against him more intimately. She hesitated but then complied. His fingers roved down her lifted arms and slowly travelled along the side of her body where he could stroke her bulging breasts now flattened against his chest.

The sound she made almost had him laughing, it was so unexpected. She squeaked like a young girl. Then she held her breath, and he knew she waited for his next move.

Truth to tell, he hadn't had this much fun since he'd been a young stud with his first girlfriend. Touching her through the silky material felt erotic as hell. The fabric moved with each stroke and created friction that pleased her, if her swaying to allow him more access was to be taken into consideration. Slowly, he caressed his way until he cupped the sides of both of her large breasts in his hands.

By the arching upwards of her body, Lucas knew she was enjoying the experience as much as he was. The instinctive movement of her lower limbs rubbing against him all but had him disgracing himself. *God! Time to call a halt!*

Again, he took her face in his hands and kissed her, his passion now leashed. He watched her expression. And he wasn't disappointed to see blissful ecstasy. When he pulled back, her lashes lifted to reveal her hunger.

By this time, her fingers had made their way down to thread through his hair and her hands gripped his head as if she needed something to hold on to. They stared at one another, roving from each other's mouths then back up to read eyes. He felt her legs caught between his and noticed his groin nestled into hers.

They'd always fit together perfectly. It had been one of the best parts about their lovemaking—how well their bodies complimented each other. In the old days, at a moment like this, Vanessa would have reached between them and boldly taken him in hand, stroking and assuming control.

Not that he had any complaints about the woman he held, cuddling close, burying her head into his shoulder. This lady-like creature pleased him, and he was just about to tell her so when the door opened and Dr. Andrews walked in.

Rolling off of him, gamely trying to get to her feet, Vanessa stuttered and hid her blushing face.

Dr. Andrews rushed forward to assist her; otherwise Vanessa would have landed on top of Lucas once again. Obviously traumatized, she wrenched her hands from the doctor's and wrapped them around her shaking body. "I fell. Lucas caught me before I hit the ground. He probably saved me from a nasty injury."

"So I see. It's a good thing he was here." Dr. Andrew's smirk and wink in her direction had Lucas wondering. Her red-faced response was even more curious. *What was this all about?*

With a harrumph, she flung herself on the bed. It was then she noticed the undeniable look of satisfaction the doctor wore. "Tobias? Why are you smiling like that?"

"I've just been to a meeting with the rest of the doctors on your case, and we've decided that since you've progressed so well, by the weekend you should be fit to leave hospital and go home." His face-splitting grin reflected his satisfaction. Lucas could now see why all the nurses deferred to this man and why his wife trusted and liked him so much. Dignified as a specialist, and debonair as a man, both traits garnered respect and affection.

"That's wonderful news, Doctor. My son will be over the moon. All he's been talking about is the day his mummy comes home."

Both men turned in time to see Vanessa slump back against the pillows, clutching the left side of her face.

Chapter 16

What was she to do? Grace laid on her bed immersed in her thoughts. Earlier in the day, when Lucas had shown such overwhelming hunger for his wife, she'd been carried away. But after they'd been interrupted by Tobias, fear such as she'd never known had attacked. What in the world had given her the idea that she could carry off this travesty? The man expected a woman in his bed who knew him intimately—his body, his likes, his fantasies. A woman versed in the art of lovemaking—someone who knew how to behave in the arms of a passionate man. All she knew how to do was hang on and be willing.

If the truth were known, she'd never experienced such utterly lovely sensations as he'd achieved with his expert hands roving her intimate areas. She could have stayed in his arms forever, learning more about what really happened between a man and a woman in the throes of passion.

It was true, she understood the technicalities. After all, she'd been a dedicated nurse for many years. But other than a dreadful experience as a young girl, losing her virginity to a nerdy type who hadn't cared about what her face looked like in the dark, she hadn't any familiarity with the art of sex. None whatsoever!

Could he tell?

Well, of course he could, you ninny!

What in the world was she to do? Acting the part of his sick wife was one thing. Using her loss of memory as a reason for her not remembering details had worked just fine. But the intimate act between a man and a woman had to be inherent, didn't it?

Since she'd partnered with Dr. Andrews, Grace had read up on the work of Sigmund Freud and Carl Jung, two pioneers in the psychiatry field. She'd found Jung's books involving the collective and personal unconscious to be particularly interesting. He believed archetypal personalities and individual traits were inbred from birth. Her question therefore had to be—could a coma destroy intuition?

Sex, being one of the strongest emotional acts, wouldn't be forgotten, would it—especially with a man like Lucas? She needed to talk to Tobias and quickly. There'd be no sleep for her until they discussed what she was to do when her husband claimed his marital rights.

Just then the man she'd been thinking about stepped into her room and carefully closed the door.

"I had a feeling you'd be wanting to talk with me, my dear. I saw the panic in your eyes earlier and waited until Lucas left before returning."

"He was full of plans about my homecoming, Tobias. He's going to bring Sammy to see me tomorrow so we can give him the good news together."

"And..."

"And he says he'll show me all around so I'll know

where everything is."

"And..."

"And we're going to buy a puppy for Sammy."

"And..." This time he crossed his arms, and his forbidding stance showed her his patience was wearing thin.

"And, he wants to make love to me. Me—Grace Joye! Not Vanessa Knight. He wants her body, yes, but he'll be getting my soul. Oh, God, Doctor, what am I going to do?"

Since the incident on the floor, tears had hovered. But now these words unhooked her control and a torrent flowed freely. She clutched her face in both hands and bent over her uplifted knees.

"Grace, lovie, what's happening 'ere? Doctor, what are you doing to this poor girl?" Mrs. Dorn bustled into the room, dropped her parcels and rushed to the bed to gather the weeping Grace into her arms.

Stuttering, Grace replied. "Lucas wants to make love to me."

"Is that all? Thank goodness for small mercies. Of course, he does, child. I've seen the way the man stares at you. The bloke's bonkers over ya. And I don't blame him none. If I were a man, I'd want ya for me own, and that's the right of it."

Dr. Andrews cleared his throat so loud that both ladies swiveled in his direction. He stood rigid, a furious look not often seen, made his face look rather red and Grace believed that even his distinguished grey hair appeared to stand at attention.

"Mrs. Dorn," he bellowed. "Mrs. Knight is my patient and we were having a consultation before you barged into the room. May I request that you step outside for a short while so that we may continue?"

Grace's attention was caught as she watched the brief war between her two champions.

"Oh, pooh! She needs a motherly shoulder for her tears, not a doctor's prescription." Mrs. Dorn's unrelenting stern expression made Dr. Andrews look from one woman to the other before snorting and backing down. Once again, Grace's streaked face sought Mrs. Dorn's ample chest while the chubby old hands soothed and stroked her hair.

"Fine, you may stay. In fact, it's probably for the best, because we need to resolve something here and we'll do it now.

"Grace, once and for all you must make up your mind if you are willing to continue as Mrs. Vanessa Knight. If you feel you can't proceed, Henrietta and I will help you start a new life in every way possible. But, you must realize"—and he emphasized *must* strongly— "that you have run out of time. It wouldn't be fair to either Lucas or Samuel for you to go to their home and then leave them after such a step. Both already love you and are willing to accept that you are who they believe you to be."

The minute he'd started to speak, she'd sat up and listened carefully. Voice tones could make a huge difference to the words spoken. After listening to this speech, Grace knew this to be true. Every word, concise and heartfelt, was engraved onto her brain and she appreciated, without a doubt, the seriousness of his directives. She looked toward Mrs. Dorn who sat nodding her head; the wart on the pale skin of her nose stood out stronger than ever and called attention to her wobbling chin and artificially reddened lips now caught between her teeth.

When she still hadn't replied, Dr. Andrews spoke again.

"If you like, I can talk to Lucas and tell him that you

are fragile, that your mental state is still seeking answers to who you are and what happened in the past. That he must be gentle and patient to help you regain some of what's been lost. He's a good man and will give you time."

Grace felt the doctor watch her closely for signs of compliance or resistance, trying to read her expression. If she still wore Grace's face, without a doubt, he'd have known what her soft heart needed. But this face was as new to him as it was to her. Thoughts filtered through her head at an alarming rate. What was she to do?

Her love for Samuel screamed for her to be the mother he coveted, the mother she knew she could be. But the fearful, unloved woman who'd lived her life hiding behind her hand, giving up dreams without a fight—that woman held her back.

Suddenly a huge wave of yearning filled every crevice inside of her until taking another breath seemed impossible. Both the doctor and Mrs. Dorn moved forward as if they sensed she needed help. Before they could do anything, the powerful sensation released her, and she fell back against the pillows, weak but resolved.

"I will be Vanessa Knight, mother and wife. And I will be a good mother, and the best wife I know how to be. Learning has always come easily to me, so I'll research everything I need, and I'll succeed."

"Bless my soul, Gracie. You had me scared for a minute. Why, one of life's greatest pleasures for a young woman is carrying on with the right man. Back in my day, I had a beau or two who tickled my—"

"Mrs. Dorn!"

"Er...fancy. Yes, well, it's a jolly good life you'll have, and we'll help you every step of the way, won't we, Doctor?"

"Absolutely, but just one more thing and then we'll not

speak of this ever again. Mrs. Dorn, once again you've called her Grace. That must stop. Now! From this minute forward, she is Vanessa Knight, Lucas's wife and Samuel's mother. Do you understand?" His demanding gaze moved from Grace to a red-faced Mrs. Dorn. "Do I make myself clear?" he asked again, his tone brooking no nonsense.

"Yes, Doctor." Tight curls bobbing around her face as she swiveled toward the bed, Mrs. Dorn said, "I'm ever so sorry, Gr...I mean, Vanessa. It won't happen again—if I can help it."

At that moment, something caught at Grace's attention and halted her movement toward Mrs. Dorn. Stopping her intention to hug the dear woman who showed her such caring, she looked toward the door, which sat open a few inches.

"Doctor, did you close the door when you came into the room?"

"Yes, I remember distinctly wanting some privacy to speak with you. Henrietta, did you close the door?" Both Grace and he turned to the perplexed housekeeper.

"I don't remember," she answered. Biting her lip, she raised her hands outwards and flopped back in her chair, making her full-skirted, red, polka-dotted dress billow around her ample girth. "Why do you ask?"

Pale and shaken, Grace answered. "I'm sure someone was at the door just now. What if they heard us talking?"

"Oh dear," said Dr. Andrews.

"Sod a dog!" said Mrs. Dorn.

Chapter 17

Mrs. Dorn sat in the visitor's chair and watched as Grace flitted around the room, gathering her personal belongings together to pack into the suitcase that Lucas had sent to the hospital earlier that morning.

"You say he didn't bring the suitcase hisself? He had the nurse deliver it? And that worries you because?"

"Because if it was Lucas who listened to us talking last night, won't he be angry and confused and want to stay away? Really, Henrietta, what must he be thinking?"

"Most likely that we're bonkers, the lot of us." Mrs. Dorn snorted, the sound so perfectly matched to the situation, it made Grace smile. "But what makes you think it was him? Or anyone for that matter? It remains to be seen whether or not you actually saw anything. Look 'ere. I reckon it's best to keep a stiff upper lip and not to worry over what ya can't change."

Before Grace could answer her friend, the door opened to reveal a happy-faced boy pulling on his father's hand. "Mummy, I'm here." As soon as he saw Grace, Samuel yanked free and ran toward her open, waiting arms. With his own arms wrapped around her middle, and his grinning cheeks against her stomach, he wore an expression of bliss. Finally, he pulled back far enough to look up. "Daddy took ever so long this morning to get ready. I waited and waited."

"Not to worry Sammy-son. You're here now." While she spoke, Grace hugged him close, her fingers filtering through the soft curls so like her own.

Being a perceptive child, he noticed that his father hadn't said anything yet. He turned with a frown to glance back at the man who still hovered near the door.

Obviously, not being a fool, Lucas took his cue, stepped into the room and came toward his wife. Once close enough, he leaned over the boy still enjoying his mother's embrace and lightly kissed her cheek. "Good morning, dear. I see you got the suitcase I sent. It's wonderful that you're packing to come home."

Grace would have felt much better if he'd have looked into her eyes while he spoke such welcoming words. It was very difficult gauging someone's reaction when their lashes hid the truth. Before this thought could go any further, he reached his big arms around his family and joined them all in a group hug.

Her relief was tremendous. *I guess I have my answer. I'll never leave these two. They are my family and even though I'm not entitled to their love, I'll do everything in my power to deserve it and them.*

The sniffle from the corner reminded everyone that Mrs. Dorn still sat in the chair, witnessing their display. Lucas motioned to Grace that he had to leave for a little while and Grace nodded in agreement. She wondered if the smile he finally allowed to break loose was in answer to her own beaming, or was his happiness as great as her own.

She couldn't be sure, but the warm caress of his large palm against her cheek started tingles flaring up everywhere. Shivers of delight had her clenching her muscles, and the flowing sensation of pleasure was welcome and wonderful after the stress she'd been suffering.

Sam waved goodbye as his dad left the room and then turned to the visitor patiently waiting.

"Hello? I'm Sam." Like the perfect little gentleman his dad had taught him to be, he moved forward, reaching to shake Mrs. Dorn's hand.

Visibly melting, she put her fingers out as if he were her subject and she was royalty. Sam, not sure what to do, played the gentleman perfectly.

"I'm Mrs. Dorn. And you're a cutie-pie, ain'tcha?"

Serious, as only a four-year-old can be when confronted by a silly question, he answered. "No, I'm a boy."

"Righto! So you are. And a fine strapping lad at that."

With his dignity restored, his small frame swelled, and his chest noticeably lifted. "My mummy's coming home tomorrow." The boy's voice held a world of smiles.

Whether it was the words or the way they were spoken, the statement was enough to shatter Mrs. Dorn's control. Tears cascaded to form two rivulets on her chubby cheeks. Her sniffles increased until she hid her face behind plump hands.

"Are you alright, Henrietta?" Grace had to accept that a grunt and vigorous nodding meant she was fine.

Sammy ran to Grace's side and hid behind her leg. "Mummy, why is the lady crying?" Uneasiness was palpable in the boy's tone.

"I think it's because she's happy."

Movement from the chair caught their attention and they watched the tight curls on the older woman's head flop around as she vigorously nodded her agreement.

"Yep. She's happy." Sam moved back to stand beside Henrietta and reached over to pat the same hand clutching tissues which had miraculously appeared from somewhere inside of her sleeve.

With a huge drawn-in breath, she glanced at him and smiled, albeit with a slight wobble around the chin. "I'm so happy for you, Grace. It's wonderful to know this angel is your son."

Sam, mystified, turned as Grace approached and whispered. "Why did Mrs. Dorn call you Grace?"

Mortified, the culprit stared at Grace who was lost for words. It felt as if the whole world stopped. Now what? Goodness, was it all over because of one little, insignificant slip? Had she lost everything?

She didn't reckon on the wiliness from a woman who'd used that trait all her life. Who'd lived by her wits many times, possibly because she'd always gotten herself in so many pickles over the years?

Mrs. Dorn chuckled. It sounded fake to Grace, but not to an innocent boy. "It's only her nickname from when I knew her before she was yer mum."

"A nickname? You mean like when my mummy calls me Sammy-son. Is that a nickname?"

When they both nodded, delight lit his face and he said, "I like Grace, but I like Mummy better." He reached into his pocket and carefully pulled out a folded sheet of paper and handed it to Grace. "I drew you a picture, and I colored it all by myself." He passed her his gift—his shining green eyes so large they seemed to swell from the sockets while his bottom lip slipped between his teeth. Then he leaned his body against hers as if he needed to be as close as possible.

Grace perused the precious item and felt everything inside her turn to pure mush. She knew the smile on her face probably looked silly but couldn't care less. What she held in her hands was the best present anyone had ever given her, and it meant the world.

Eyes glittery with affection, she looked down and asked, "Did you sign your own name to this masterpiece?"

Proudly, he nodded. "Daddy told me the letters, but I printed them."

Mrs. Dorn, not being able to wait another second, stood up and peered over Grace's shoulder. The picture he'd drawn was of two adults both holding the hand of a small boy in the middle. They stood in front of a house with a large tree high on the opposite corner.

The woman, who Grace supposed was her, had yellow squiggles around her head, huge green eyes and wore a full-skirted pink dress. Dark slashes around the man's head, which obviously was his hair, surrounded an oval face with owl-like eyes that looked a bit comical, but held a surprisingly humorous stare. She saw a darker smudge mark where he'd erased his work in order to redo the image he'd wanted, and it was endearing to think he had a vision he'd wanted to perfect.

Grace noticed a small round creature whose head peered around the base of the tree. She pointed there and asked, "Who's this fellow, Sam?"

"It's my puppy. Daddy said after you were settled at home we might go and find me a mate, and so I drew him into the picture. That's okay, isn't it?"

Grace heard the worry and quickly soothed him.

"It's perfect. We'll put a trip to the dog shelter on our list of outings as something we can all do together. And we'll find you the best little puppy you ever dreamed of."

Not being able to help herself, she bent down and gathered him in her arms to hug his little body close. Awash with affection, she felt stunned when an even greater force filled her to the point where she became afraid she'd swoon. Quickly, she pulled away and stood up, a little frightened by the experience.

The boy breathed an audible sigh of relief and moved to throw himself on the bed, happiness lighting his face, reminding her of a child on Christmas morning after sighting zillions of presents under a tree.

Chapter 18

Lucas had to leave the room. He couldn't stay there and watch the woman who'd stolen his heart yet again play a role he now suspected was a sham.

Words he'd overheard as he'd hovered in the doorway last night returned to haunt him.

According to Mrs. Dorn, his wife's name was Grace. And Dr. Andrews had warned the culprit she must never use that name again. What were the exact words? Oh, yes! *"From this minute forward, she is Vanessa Knight, Lucas's wife and Samuel's mother. Do you understand?"* Even though he'd been hidden, he'd heard 'non-negotiable' stressed in Dr. Andrew's tone. The doctor had meant what he said and was to be obeyed.

Lucas stopped walking and leaned his large body against the wall, his hands covering his face. How could her name be Grace? And where had she known the old housekeeper from? He knew Vanessa had never introduced him to anyone from her past, so was it possible that Mrs. Dorn knew her from an earlier time? Could it be during that time she'd been known as Grace?

Vanessa had always refused to talk about those years. All he knew was that she'd been born to a low-income family who'd lived on the outskirts of London. He'd been led to believe her parents were both dead and she was an only child. She'd always shied away from any personal discussions. When he'd reminisced about his happy childhood, she'd listened and smiled, but would say nothing of her own upbringing.

Except for her time at college where she'd taken her master's degree in Art History. She had talked about those days.

Wait, there was that one time when they'd been viewing a pottery exhibition, and she'd let it out that she'd wanted to be a potter. He seemed to remember her admitting that she couldn't follow her dream because of an injury in her right hand that hadn't healed properly; she didn't have the strength needed to work in that medium. After searching out different careers, she'd found a hidden talent for art restoration. The famous gallery who'd employed her in London had assigned their most treasured collectibles to be restored by Vanessa Grey. She had the hands of a true perfectionist, a conservationist marvel.

Get real, Lucas. His mind caught him up. She must have had some acquaintances from those years. Why couldn't Mrs. Dorn be one of them? It was possible.

"Mr. Knight. Has something happened?" Dr. Hoven quick-stepped toward Lucas, worry stamped on his features.

Standing tall, Lucas ignored the tightness in his stomach and turned to the doctor. "It's my wife! There's something I can't explain about her. She's different." He didn't intend to share his thoughts with the man, but the pounding in his head meant his usual controls had slipped.

Guiding him to seats in an open office, Dr. Hoven sat next to Lucas and crossed one leg over the other as if this relaxed stance would calm the other man. Surprisingly, Lucas felt the hard edge seep away and his normal composure return.

"Now what's this about Mrs. Knight changing? And what, may I ask, do you believe is different?"

Everything inside him wanted to hide the facts he needed to share, but common sense kicked in before discretion took over. "Look, Dr. Hoven. Mrs. Knight has always been a rather cold woman, introverted and self-contained, if you will." Pointing toward the direction of her room, Lucas continued. "This version is the complete opposite. You've seen how she lights up with everyone and how soft-spoken and—well—kind she is. Trust me, Doctor, my wife didn't like other people before, and in no uncertain terms let it show."

"You're saying her personality has undergone a change?"

"More than a change. It's as if she's a whole different person. I know it sounds ridiculous, but my instincts tell me she's not who we believe. Hell, she doesn't even kiss the same way." Whatever had made him blurt out that last part, he'd never know; probably frustration?

Dr. Hoven chuckled. "Is that all? You had me worried there for a minute. It's a well-known phenomenon that people can undergo personality changes while locked in a coma. Many in our profession accept that the patient's brain is functioning, but at a somewhat lower level. Doesn't mean to say they are fully aware of everything around them, only that some recall filtering memories, hearing voices and making—shall we say—promises with a higher being to be better people if given another chance."

"You don't understand, she's not the same in any way other than her appear—"

"No, *you* don't understand. You must be patient. Certain habits are ingrained. As time goes on, when you're back home and she's in her own setting, you'll see those familiar mannerisms. The hospital is like a foreign country where everything is unique and dissimilar."

"Fine, I accept that. But how do you explain her new love for Samuel? Before the car crash, she hated the sight of the boy. Wouldn't be in the same room with him, or even say goodnight to him even after he asked for her repeatedly. And not an hour before she drove her vehicle so dangerously as to end up in an accident, I caught her beating him. Now, she's warm and loving, a mother every child would be fortunate to have. Explain that to me." Lucas sat forward with his hands clenched between his legs. Embarrassment for his bluntness made him look everywhere but at the man whose uncontrolled exclamation still hung in the air.

Clearing his voice, Dr. Hoven also leaned forward, no longer looking or acting quite so cocky. "I'm afraid this isn't quite my area of expertise, Mr. Knight. You'd be better off asking these questions of Dr. Andrews. He seems to know your wife quite well and would, I'm sure, have a much better insight into her behavioral problems than I."

"Then there's one area you can help me with. Sometime in the past, my wife had an injury to her hand that stopped her from being a potter, which was her dream. During the accident, wasn't there some damage to her right hand and didn't you have to operate?"

"Yes, now that you mention it, we did. There were unset

broken bones in her hand, which fortunately, we were able to repair. In fact, there were other wounds healed over that hadn't been dealt with properly either, one in her arm and others in her shoulder area. At the time, we'd wondered if she'd been in an accident as a child."

Just then they heard an announcement. "Dr. Hoven to Theatre Three." With a pat on Lucas's shoulder, the doctor rushed from the room.

Lucas leaned back in the chair and rubbed his stomach. *There's the proof you needed, old chap.* She was Vanessa. Except that his sixth sense told him the woman in the room down the hall, the one he'd begun to adore and want more than he wanted his next breath, was the complete opposite from the wife he used to know and hated.

Chapter 19

"And this is your new bedroom, Mummy." Sammy couldn't contain his excitement at having his mother back home. He chattered like a crazed magpie and didn't walk a step, but scampered everywhere.

"It's a new bedroom?" Grace gazed at the lovely pearl tones of the coral walls. It was her favorite color, one she wore a lot. Windows, decorated with filmy sheers on each side, overlooked the back of the house screening a vista of huge trees and flowering shrubs in the distance. A comfy window seat guaranteed a favorite place for her to read the vast array of romance books she devoured. Dark furniture and a light carpet added to the atmosphere of tranquility and Grace instantly felt right at home.

Lucas entered, carrying her suitcase and a plant from the hospital. "Where would you like these?" He laid the suitcase on the hand-quilted, flower-print cover that made the bed look so homey, then lifted the plant toward her, indicating it specifically.

Shyness attacked, and she cupped her left cheek without thinking. "How about on this small table," she said, pointing to a lovely antique near the window.

Straightening after doing her bidding, he glanced around the room and then turned to her. "So, what do you think?"

"I think it's lovely. Sam says it's a new room? But I'm not sure what that means?" Ensconced on the window seat, the boy paid no attention to the adults, or so it seemed. Grace recognized his stance and knew he listened.

"During one of the sessions I had with Dr. Andrews, he explained how your memory of the past had deteriorated and that we must ease you back into your old life. He felt that rather than resume our... ah... marriage activities, we must let you take your time and settle in slowly. So, I've had the housekeeper move your clothes and most of your personal articles into this room for the time being. We did a bit of a brush-up with paint and new furniture."

"How thoughtful you are, Lucas. I'm sure I'll be very happy here, especially if I get lots of visits." Desire flared in his searching gaze, desire he didn't try to hide, and it was his expression—arched eyebrows and cheeky grin—that made her aware of how her words could be misconstrued. "I-I mean visits from Sam." Stricken, she gulped and purposely moved toward the boy as if for protection.

Hearing his name, Sam bolted over to her side. "Are you sick, Mum? Your face is all red."

Lucas's chuckle broke the tension and she laughed. "I'm fine, Sammy-son. Just happy to be here with you. Now, how about taking me on a tour of the rest of the house? Dr. Andrews was right. I have no memory of the place whatsoever and I wouldn't want to get lost. I don't think I've ever been in such a beautiful home."

"You used to say it was ugly and—and too big."

The child wasn't being confrontational. He just

repeated words he'd heard. And they made Grace's heart sore. From what she'd seen of the place, it was fit for a queen. Remodeled homes were tricky. Many times, the architects ruined the gracious elegance by tampering with the initial styles and trying to make a house more modern. From what she'd seen, Lucas had combined the two perfectly, which left a home so classy it should make anyone proud.

The silence finally cut off her musings and she became aware both males had stopped, wearing shocked expressions.

"Mummies can be wrong sometimes too, Sam. I've changed my mind. I think our house is perfect and that your daddy is a genius."

She caught the pleased surprise Lucas couldn't hide, and a wonderful feeling of happiness spread throughout her body as he reached out his hand. She took it and then reached out her own for Sam. "Right, gentlemen, show me the castle."

***

After a lovely meal served by Lucas's housekeeper, before the keen-eyed woman left for the night, Grace noticed that the excitement of Sam's day had exhausted the little boy. He barely finished his small plate of roast beef before his eyelids began to droop. Her offering to be the one to read his stories and help him get ready for bed re-ignited his animation, though getting him to finally settle took two stories, a glass of milk and many cuddles.

Lucas, worn out, had finally given way and let Grace take over with the excuse that he'd make tea. Once she left the boy's bedroom, Lucas called her to join him in the den for a welcome cuppa.

He passed her a delicate flowered bone china cup and

saucer, and then sat near her on the same sofa.

"Vanessa, I'm sorry for leaving you with the infant tornado. It's your first day home. You should be in bed yourself." Grace had noticed how he'd lingered; never leaving them alone for long until finally he couldn't deny how happy she and Samuel were in each other's company.

"I'm fine. The nap this afternoon worked wonders. He can't help it, Lucas. He's just a little boy."

"He's a monster whose been hiding all these years. I've never known him to get so excited or be so vocal. He hasn't stopped chattering all day long."

"Yes. Isn't it wonderful? He has such a lively mind, and he's very intelligent. The questions he asks? Goodness! I never knew four-year-olds were so smart."

"Smart-assed, you mean. The crafty little nipper has you twisted around his baby finger; you know that, don't you?"

"Wonderful, isn't it? I've never been loved so beautifully."

Silence spread and had her re-thinking her words. She'd felt that comfortable, they'd just popped out. Finally, she couldn't stand the stress another minute and set her teacup down, preparing to excuse herself.

Before she could, he'd placed his saucer on the table also and grabbed her hand, forcing her to sit again. Then he leaned over and took her face between his large, gentle hands, disarming her with a searching glance that brooked no silliness.

His hold was too firm for her to pull away gracefully. Dreading an interrogation, she wanted to be gone. *Why is he forcing me to be rude?* Knowing it wasn't in her nature to hurt anyone's feelings, especially someone she cared for, she closed her eyes, held her breath and waited.

"At one time, if I'd have tried to hold you against your

will, you would have smacked me and left."

That had her eyes popping open real quick. *Now what do I say?* Hesitating, she eventually decided to be herself. "I've changed, Lucas. I don't know who I am anymore." There! That should satisfy the interrogator.

"I don't know who you are either, but I like you and I want to keep you."

His smiling lips touched hers softly. She felt the tip of his tongue prod her lips to open, and wanting to feel what it would be like to really kiss a man, she relaxed. Quick as a wink, he invaded, teasingly licking the inside of her mouth before adding pressure. It was completely devastating. One minute she was fully conscious of every sensation and the next, a whirlwind of emotion had overcome her restraints and she fell into an abyss of wanting—wanting his hands and lips everywhere on her body. Trembling, every womanly part in her body screaming for fulfillment, she opened herself and followed where he took her.

He used his mouth like a brilliant surgeon controlling a scalpel. He played with her. First his lips devastated and then he withdrew slightly, which only had her whimpering her dismay. Then he re-angled his head and resumed the passionate assault until she was consumed with desire and clung with a dizzying kind of panic that he'd stop altogether.

Of their own accord, her hands lifted to rake through his hair and when she sensed he'd pull away, she clutched his head. Never having touched a man in such a personal way, she wanted the moment to last forever.

When he gently pushed her backwards to lie on the sofa, she accommodated him the best she could, lying crookedly in order for him to have space. When his hands began to stroke her hair, she lifted her head so he had access. And when his mouth made love to her neck, she arched this way and that, so he was able to reach every inch of her sensitized skin. She never knew the vortex of passion was so beautiful.

Hungrily, his lips worked their way to the top of her dress where only a few buttons, easily opened, had kept him from finding her breasts. His adept fingers had no trouble undoing that which kept him from his goal, and soon his mouth attacked the large mounds of flesh, the nipples hardened and responsive.

One minute his tongue wreaked havoc on her body while his moans increased her own need, and in the next, a loud groan broke free as he wrenched himself from her arms and slid to the floor. He slumped against the side of the sofa with his head in his hands, dejection like a halo around his slumped shoulders.

"I'm sorry, Van. We can't do this. Dr. Andrews forbids any lovemaking until he's finished assessing your case; some hogwash about upsetting your conceptual core and damaging your mental acuity."

What?!! Bloody hell! As soon as she stopped her inner cussing—a new habit she'd picked up while spending so much time with Mrs. Dorn—she realized that Tobias was only trying to protect her, but right then she wished him and his protectiveness in purgatory.

Lucas's husky voice interrupted her inner wailing. "I can't wait to get you into our bed again. Have you make love to me in that special way." Overcome by emotion, he stopped to clear his throat. "It's the proof I need to really believe you're my wife, the woman I once loved."

His eyes searched her own, his sultry with passion unfulfilled. The only thought in her mind was—*don't look away. Don't show fear. Oh God...Lucas, don't hate me.*

"I told you I can't remember anything about what I used to do." How she hated the lies.

"Don't worry, darling. You also told me once it was instinctive. Never, in all the times we had together did you ever forget."

As he spoke, he watched her expressions change. She knew dismay crowded out the earlier joy.

His eyes narrowed, and his hands formed into fists. "Nothing in the world will convince me that you're my wife if you've forgotten the one beautiful thing we always shared. And no matter how difficult it would be tearing you away from Sam, you'll be out of this house with no chance of ever returning."

In a graceful move, his sinuous body rose, and he strode to the door, hesitated and looked back at her. "Don't be fooled, Van," he sneered, "—and might I remind you of how much you hated that nickname. To save Sam further heartache, I'd cut you out of our lives like I'd cut off a poisonous tumor."

Chapter 20

Immediately after he left her sight, Lucas's shoulders slumped, and he slowed to a stumbling gait. *How could I have been so cruel?* Just for a second, he thought about returning, apologizing and telling her had hadn't meant what he'd said. That frustration and anger had taken over his senses.

But, how could he?

Everything inside him screamed that this sweetheart of a lady was an imposter—a lovely imposter. But there was no denying the fact that the more time he spent in her company, the more certain he became that she couldn't be his dispassionate, brutal wife.

This Vanessa looked a person straight in the eyes, albeit shyly, but with a composure unknown to the old Vanessa who, during the last four years, had reverted to acting more like a sullen teenager than a grown woman.

He kept asking himself the same question over and over. How could a person change so drastically? Everything except their looks? Wracked with guilt for leaving her so devastated, he tried to think of anyone who had known her well before the accident.

It was his need for drink that made him think of the bartender in the place across from the hospital. Should he go? Could he leave the boy with her, alone and unprotected?

The memory of her behavior on the day of the accident haunted him continually and he knew, as a father, it had been his responsibility to protect his child from being terrorized, to protect him from the bad guy, even if in this case that had happened to be the child's own mother.

Lucas went up the stairs to the rear of the house and knocked on the nanny's door. Flora Grieve, Sam's nanny, had promised to be at home tonight. Many times she'd come in the back way and go directly to her private apartment. Her working hours were during the day, while Lucas was at the office. But while he was home, he took over Sam's care as much as he could and left the older woman to rest.

"Aye, I'm coming, Lucas. Ye can stop with the banging." Lucas had noticed that the Scottish brogue seemed more apparent when the woman became weary.

She opened the door and waited. Tall, straight-backed and with a no-nonsense way about her, the woman had saved his sanity recently. With Vanessa in the hospital and Sam needing so much positive reinforcement, this gem of a nanny had stepped in and sorted them out easily.

"Flora, do you mind opening your monitor for Sam's room? I'll be stepping out for an hour or so and I'll want you to go to him if he wakes. His mother is here, she left the hospital today, but she's quite tired and might not hear if he calls."

"Of course. I'll be looking after the pet." Flora turned to the wall by the door and twisted a button which would allow her to hear any noise that came from her charge's room. Lucas had installed the device when she'd first come to stay, and it worked very well. "Go about your business and don't be worrying none. The lad'll be fine."

Lucas explained. "With his mother arriving today, Sam couldn't contain himself. I have to admit to being happy seeing him act so normal for once that I didn't try to curb his enthusiasm. Therefore, when my wife put him to bed, he went to sleep still all wound up."

"He's just a wee lad and an occasional day of overdoing things won't be harmful a'tall. You go ahead now, and I'll listen for the laddie." First her hands made a shooing motion, and then she slowly closed the door.

Lucas still couldn't believe how lucky he'd been to find Mrs. Grieve and have her agree to take on the nanny position. He'd heard about her from a co-worker who'd hired her years ago for his own family. Then George had gotten a chance at a job in America and Mrs. Grieve hadn't considered accompanying them because her daughter and family lived in Scotland. The only way that Lucas had talked her into agreeing to take on Sam was by promising her round-trip tickets to visit Glasgow every six weeks.

Unfortunately, the trip home tired the older woman. Sometimes it took her days to get back her vitality, and even though Sam often seemed quiet for a four-year-old, he did have a lot of energy. Some days it worried Lucas. Because of her age, the older woman would hold him back from the physical outings a little boy so desperately needed. She focused more on the easier activities. Guess he couldn't blame her, between her arthritis and plain old age; she couldn't get around like a young person anymore.

***

"Good ter see you again, mate. What'll ya be drinking

this fine night?" Other than a few blokes sitting at one table in the back, the friendly bar was empty. The bewhiskered bartender seemed happy to see Lucas and held out his hand to greet him as he approached the scuffed, oak-topped counter. Like all good innkeepers worth their salt, he was drying glasses with a rather soiled dishtowel when Lucas arrived, but put the rag down quite happily.

He waited until Lucas had seated himself on one of the barstools and stood with his bushy eyebrow raised.

"Right, I'll have a beer. And one for yourself—my treat."

"I don't mind if I do." The big man moved agilely in the small space, and in no time, two large mugs of beer sat foaming with condensation quickly gathering on the glass.

His rheumy eyes felt like lasers as they searched Lucas's face. "Yer wife is home now, I hear." He stated it. No question there.

"And how would you know that?" Lucas said, teasing just a little.

"I went over there to give the poor lass the benefit of me charmin' company, and they said she'd gone home today. Surprised me, it did. I wouldn'ta thought she'd get better so quickly."

Lucas had to think about that for a few seconds and realized it was after he'd taken Sam to see her that she'd really driven herself to get better.

"I guess it was our son who spurred her on. After he visited, she pushed hard to get back her strength."

"Well, the boy always did mean a lot to her. Like I told ya before, she looked at his picture all the time. Even bragged about him after a few drinks. Didn't happen too often, but on those nights, she'd be happy to tell anyone who'd listen about her wonderful family. We became chums, if'n ya know what I mean. Funny thing is though—when I went to see her in the hospital, she didn't remember me at all."

"The doctors called it retrograde amnesia. Means she suffered a head injury in the accident, which is likely the cause of her memory loss."

"What struck me funny, and this is just me, mind ya, the lady I visited had a completely different way about her. My old customer's eyes never shone the way this lady's did. She never was one to laugh. Now I'll not be sayin' she didn't have a sense of humor, but she showed it more in her expression than an out and out laugh, if'n ya get me drift."

Lucas sat upright on his stool and watched every nuance in the barkeeper's expression. He didn't want to miss a word. "And the Vanessa you visited in the hospital? What was your impression of her?"

"A comely lass, with a heart of gold. She acted delighted that I came to visit. Apologized for not remembering me. And promised to stop by and lift a glass with me once she was able to celebrate her recovery. We had a lovely visit."

"Specifically, what made you think she'd changed?" Lucas needed confirmation that he wasn't crazy or imagining things.

"Ya know, it wasn't any one thing. I don't know if I can explain what I believe. And don't be thinking me crazy if I tell you what popped into my mind as I sat by her side."

Lucas waved away the suggestion that he would do any such thing. Despite his concern, he lifted his mug to the big man whose expression showed his deep thoughts. The twinkle had been replaced with a seriousness not often revealed.

"The aura around our girl shone golden and bright,

rather than sad and dark. Not sure if that'll make any sense to you, but me mother was a firm believer in auras and taught me to take note."

A bit of red filtered through the scruffy beard and made Lucas realize his friend had been deadly serious. The Irish beliefs were possibly quaint, but nonetheless feasible. At least in this instant! Because the words had described exactly how Lucas had been feeling himself: golden and bright versus sad and dark.

Lucas answered, wanting to pacify his companion. "My mother's an Irish colleen, from Dublin, so don't worry about me thinking you're foolish. As a child, I went to sleep listening to the Irish legends, all wonderful tales. My favorites were about fairies and the little people."

"Ya don't say now? I'll be from Dublin me self. Well, that demands a celebration. The next is on me." Agile as a young man in his prime, the happy fellow reached for two clean mugs and held them to the beer tap until full to the brim. He placed one in front of Lucas, lifted his and waited.

Once the custom had been observed, Lucas unapologetically wangled the conversation back to his wife.

"You said you found this Vanessa to be more likable—"

"I didn't say that, lad. I said she was happier and I found that to be different. I quite liked your wife before the accident. She broke me heart with her suffering, but she always acted like a lady to me."

Chapter 21

Grace heard the boy's cries. They sounded far away but, as a nurse, her ears were tuned to calls of distress. She rolled from under the warm bedcovers, grabbed her housecoat from the nearby chair and made her way in the dark down the hall. Having put the lad to bed earlier, she knew which room he occupied and went directly there.

His night light conjured weird shadows everywhere around the walls, but she easily made out the bed where Sammy tossed and turned. Without hesitation, she flew to his side and lit the Mickey Mouse lamp on his bedside table. Then she gathered him to her gently and crooned in a low, melodic voice.

He quieted instantly. "Mummy?"

"Yes, darling, Mummy's here. Everything is fine, Sammy-son. You were having a bit of an upset."

He wrapped his arms around her neck and squeezed tightly. "I'm sorry for being such a bad boy, Mummy. Please don't hate me." Still half asleep, his words were clear but made no sense.

Just then another woman appeared in the open

doorway, but Grace couldn't acknowledge her until she'd answered the boy who nestled close as possible.

"Of course I don't hate you, Sammy-son. I love you."

"But I'm a bad boy." Persistent, the child, still half asleep, seemed to feel strongly about this one thing.

Just as persistent, Grace was determined to erase whatever ghastly memory he clung to.

"If once you were a bad boy Sam, I forgive you. We never have to speak of it again, so forget it ever happened. From now on, just remember, I love you dearly."

He pushed away from her close embrace, wiped the tears gathered on his lashes and stared intently into her face. "Always, Mummy, will you always love me, no matter what?"

"Always, Sammy-son! No matter what."

She kissed his forehead and with a gentle touch, she pushed his sweaty bangs to the side. Her words obviously soothed his anxiety. He leaned back against her breasts and, with a loud sigh, closed his eyes. Seconds later, he was asleep. Conscious of the figure still hovering in the doorway, Grace waited for only a few moments before laying the boy down and straightening his covers to pull them over his shoulders. She leaned down and kissed the pudgy cheek, shut off the bedside light and tiptoed toward the hall.

After swinging the door partially closed, she turned to the older woman wrapped in a dark green chenille housecoat.

"You must be Sam's nanny?" she whispered. In accord, they began to move toward the staircase, past stained-glass windows embellishing the hallway, and into the den where they both took seats facing each other.

Conscious that the frilly, peachy-pink colored

housecoat of Mrs. Dorn's choice looked quite frivolous next the utilitarian one worn by the solemn-faced woman frowning at her over her spectacle rims, Grace tried to relax. But it set her at a disadvantage and she squirmed while trying to keep the slippery silk from sliding open. Finally settled, she smiled at Sam's nanny, hoping she looked less nervous than she felt. The woman's sour face could make an angel twitch.

"Well, of course I'm the nanny. After all, I've been with your family since before Samuel was born."

"Samuel?" For a minute Grace didn't know who she meant. Not until his nanny glared at her foolishness. "Right! Samuel. I never think of him that way, it just seems like such an old name for a little boy."

"I agree. But it was you who insisted he be called by the name in the first place. The only person who shortened his name was your husband." The look worn by Mrs. Grieve let Grace know that she wasn't a person to be trifled with.

"I'm sorry, I don't remember. Maybe my husband explained my circumstances to you; that I can't recall anything that happened before I woke up in the hospital after the accident? In fact, I don't recollect you or your name. I've only heard you referred to as Nanny."

"My name is Flora, Mrs. Flora Grieve."

Grace felt herself flinch from Mrs. Flora Grieve's searching glower. *Goodness, she's an old tarter. I wonder what Mrs. Dorn will think of her?* Seconds passed as she tried to decide what to say. Finally, she chose to be herself, and to the devil with the real Vanessa and her silly ways.

"I'm very happy to meet you, Flora. Sammy is a wonderful child, smart and funny and very loving. I'm sure how he behaves can be directly attributed to your fine care."

Grace watched Flora visibly melt. A smile formed and changed her appearance completely. Across from her now sat a relaxed person who seemed willing to be friends. "You do look wonderful, Mrs. Knight. I don't think I've ever seen you so relaxed and happy. I watched as you handled the incident upstairs with Samuel... Sammy, and you did everything perfectly. He'll sleep the rest of the night."

"Does he often have nightmares?"

"Since your accident, he's had many, some nights more than one. I don't know what happened that day, but it seems to be eating at the child. He's carried a huge weight around on his small shoulders, and it had to do with you being injured. I get the feeling that he blames himself."

"Surely not!" Grace couldn't stand the thought of the poor baby thinking he was responsible for an adult's disgraceful actions. She'd heard the rumors about Vanessa Knight's attempt at suicide. The police had asked her numerous questions after she'd revived, and to all of them, she'd had no answers. Finally, they'd left her alone, but not until she'd been made to understand that she'd broken the law.

Mrs. Grieve cut into her memories. "I'm hoping now that you're better, he'll let go of whatever bothered him. Some nights, he'd cry himself to sleep and he refused to settle for either me or Lucas." Shaking her head sorrowfully, Flora's features wore an emotional look of concern for her ward. This alone broke down the last of Grace's resistance, and she leaned forward to grasp the hands of the working woman.

"We'll make sure of it. From now on, I'll be the one to go to his room at night and settle his fears. Also, I hope I'll be allowed to join in your activities during the day. If

I step over your boundaries, you're to tell me. Otherwise, I'd love to take some of his more physical activities off your capable shoulders, so you'll be able to rest a little more."

"I'm tired today because I've been to Scotland to visit my daughter and grandchildren, and they are quite a handful—the children, not my daughter, although she does have her moments." Flora smiled away any seriousness.

"What a long day you've had. Please, my dear. I'll keep an ear open for Sammy. Go to bed and don't worry." Grace patted the hands she held and let them go, then stood to show the other their interlude was over.

"Mrs. Knight..."

"Please call me Vanessa."

"Vanessa, you're different, happier. And I'm very glad. But don't think I won't be keeping an eye on you until I can see that the change is here permanent."

"I wouldn't have it any other way, Flora."

Chapter 22

Over the next few days, Grace was aware that her new family watched her carefully, as if they felt it was inevitable that she would revert to a different kind of behavior. Rather daunted, she tried as hard as she could to help them relax. When the mulish, industrious housekeeper, Mrs. Platt, tiptoed into her room, she'd chat with her, trying to put her at ease. When Flora had chastised Sam to hush in her presence and not talk so loud, Grace ruffled his hair, smiled at the gruff woman and said, "It's fine. He's only having fun. I like to hear him laugh."

And when Lucas came home from work to be greeted with a calm household, she was well aware that he breathed a sigh of relief. As each day passed, everyone settled into a routine of cheerful detachment.

Everyone except Grace. She'd envisioned her life as mother to a small active boy would be busy, filled to the brim with activities. So far, that hadn't been the case at all. His routine was strictly adhered to by his nanny, and when Grace had approached Lucas about wanting to spend more time with Sam, he'd looked stern, explained that they had a set routine and it worked well. What he didn't say—but she'd plainly heard—was, *don't interfere.*

Other than the first night when she'd met Sam's nanny and seen a glimpse of her lighter side, Flora displayed a stoic front, pleasant enough, but they were all aware that when it came to her charge, she would brook no interference or foolishness of any kind. She withstood friendly overtures kindly but firmly, and changed nothing. Therefore, Grace knew her place and, so far, had been unwilling to step over the clearly marked boundaries.

As the days sped by, she acknowledged that her bedroom had become her haven and her books a solace. This boring routine had begun to irritate her. Despite her everyday walks and exercise rituals, she needed something more—something to keep her occupied. Living inside a healthy body chockablock full of energy, Grace, who'd always filled her days with hard work, now felt unneeded—useless, bored and, even worse, lonely.

Thankfully, today Henrietta planned to visit, and Grace walked on tenterhooks. Anyone who knew Henrietta Dorn was aware that boundaries meant nothing to her. *Maybe this isn't such a good idea, having her come here. I could have suggested we meet at the restaurant and have tea.*

For the last hour, Grace had been prancing from window to window, watching for the bus on the corner to discharge her best friend—the woman whose heart was as big as her overweight size.

Hands clenched into fists, she flopped onto the sofa. *Flora had better behave toward Henrietta.* This notion had stuck in her brain and wouldn't be dislodged. Her nerves were a mess; all mangled together like a bowl of cooked spaghetti.

If only there were chores for me. What in the world did

the real Vanessa spend her time on? Being beautiful was fine and good, but heavens, did it take up her whole day?

Suddenly the outer bell rang. Startled, Grace lurched, then clutched at her heart. She raced to the front door, yelling out uncharacteristically, "I'll get it!"

As soon as she'd opened the door and got swept up in a huge hug, she breathed easier. Somewhat overpowering, the smell of lilacs made her eyes water and her heart zing with affection. "Henrietta! I'm so happy to see you. Please come in and let me take your cape."

Lifting it from the woman, she hid a tiny smile in the wool of the dazzling hot-pink, massive hand-knitted garment. Mrs. Dorn was a wonderful knitter. No one would ever disparage her ability, but on the other hand, her choice of color and style left a lot to be desired.

"Gr-Vanessa, you live in a flaming mansion. Why didn't you tell me, pet? I'd've worn me better dress, rather than this ole rag." Like an actress on stage, Mrs. Dorn majestically brushed her hand against the silk skirt of her white and black polka-dotted dress, which Grace knew was her newest frock, since she'd raved about the fantastic sale she'd been to while Grace had lain in the hospital. The old housekeeper's bouncing curls were testament to a visit at the hairdressers and her rouged cheeks and red lips a signal that she'd spent a fair amount of time on her presentation.

"You look lovely, Henrietta. Truly! I'm ever so happy to see you. It's been rather quiet, and I'm going a bit stir-crazy." Grace cupped the chubby face, kissed the reddened cheek, then flung her arms around the substantial shoulders and clung.

Squeezed and petted, she felt hugely better once the greetings were dealt with. That was, until Mrs. Dorn held her at arms' reach and scrutinized her in such a way that only Mrs. Dorn could.

"Now out with it, what's the matter?"

"Nothing really." Grace tried on a happy smile. With her arm around the other woman, she guided them toward her favorite room, the wainscoted den, where the huge wall of sash windows let in the brightness from a sunny day.

"Rubbish! Do you take me for a daft old woman wearing blinders? I can see you're unhappy, and I'm not even used to yer new face. It's that flaming clear. Come on now and tell Henrietta what bothers ya."

"I'm fine, really." Grace upped the wattage of her smile and added a nod for good measure.

Mrs. Dorn's eyes became slits as she stared Grace down.

"Don't worry, my dear." Grace pointed to the most comfortable sofa and waited for Henrietta to sit.

"Uh huh!" Refusing to take the hint, the stubborn woman stood with her hands held open, as if she expected someone to pass her something.

"Oh, for heaven's sake! Have it your way then. I'm a trifle bored."

"A trifle?"

"No. You're right. I'm horribly bored and I don't know what to do about it." After she'd shared her dilemma, a thousand tons of glumness lifted off Grace's shoulders. She threw herself onto the sofa and her friend sat near her.

Taking her time, Mrs. Dorn placed her hand-knitted handbag on the table next to her and gathered her skirts close. Then she folded her hands.

"Did you ask yer handsome husband what you used to do before the accident?"

"Yes. He said that Vanes—"

Mrs. Dorn smacked Grace's hand and held up a finger,

her expression comically warning.

Grace grinned conspiratorially. "He said that *I* often went shopping. I can attest to that after seeing the contents of her...*my* various wardrobes. I also had weekly appointments at beauty salons for manicures and..." With a graceful movement, Grace flipped her hair back over her shoulder to make a point. She loved it this length; she'd always wanted long hair, but hers had been too thin to grow so she'd been forced to keep it relatively short. "The rest of my time was spent in my studio out back. Appears I'd made quite a name for myself as an artist who restored famous works of art. In fact, the gallery where I'd been employed contacted me as soon as I returned home. You'll understand that I used my loss of memory and explained that those skills have disappeared." Grace felt the sickness again in her stomach that she'd experienced each time she'd fibbed. "Henrietta, I've always hated lying. Now it seems to me this new life is all one big lie." Grace couldn't help the sigh that escaped, or her shoulders from hunching over unconsciously.

"Well this is a ruddy big mess. Nuthin we can't fix though, dearie. Give over now. Straighten up, and we'll figure out your next step."

Grace sat tall and waited. Deliberately, she lifted her hair and tossed it toward the back and then cupped the gathered curls, loving the feel of the silken mass.

Finally, Mrs. Dorn spoke. "Nursing's all you know or care about, right? Therefore, it's plain as the nose on yer face: you need to enroll in nursing. With everything you already know, you'll jolly well ace the courses and be back on the wards in no time."

Happiness exploded inside Grace. Like a rice pot boiling over, flooding everywhere, she felt hope expand. She clapped her hands together. "Why Henrietta, you're a genius. I'll tell Lucas that after my stay in the hospital, I want to devote my attention to helping those less fortunate. Do you think he'll buy it?"

"No reason why he wouldn't. After all, it's the truth, and unless he's blind as a bat and daft as well, he'll see it on your pretty face."

A squeak near the door heralded that someone had just lifted the handle. Grace raised her hand toward Mrs. Dorn in warning and they both waited as the door slowly opened. Sam's head poked around, and he held his finger to his lips, grinned like any cheeky four-year-old, and then tiptoed into the room to hide behind the open door.

In seconds they heard footsteps passing and the nanny's voice, low and annoyed, calling for Samuel. The two women sitting together saw the pleading look and both pretended not to know where he lurked, when Flora poked her head into the room.

"Excuse me, Mrs. Knight. It seems that young Samuel has decided to play hide-and-seek during his snack time and I've lost him. You wouldn't happen to know where he might be hiding, now, would you?"

Ignoring the question, not wanting to out-and-out lie, Grace motioned the woman into the room. "Flora, I'd like to introduce you to a very dear friend of mine, Mrs. Henrietta Dorn. She's housekeeper for Dr. Robert Andrews, my psychiatrist. Henrietta, this is Samuel's nanny, Mrs. Flora Grieve."

Nanny Flora nodded like a queen, looked around the room and ignored Henrietta's outstretched hand. Grace, not sure if she'd done it on purpose or just hadn't seen the gesture, experienced a tightening of her stomach.

If Mrs. Dorn had been a dog, she'd be growling. Instead,

she waved the extended hand and bit out the words, "Sam is quite the lad, Mrs. Grieve. He must be a handful for an ole woman like yerself?"

Oh, dear lord! Henrietta's back was up. Grace knew it and flinched, preparing to get between the two women if necessary.

Mrs. Grieve's gimlet stare and rude shrug betrayed the nonchalance of someone who felt rather safe in their position of power. "Not at all. He's lively but knows his manners and would never be naughty on purpose, or play mean tricks on his old nanny."

Crafty, thought Grace, who wasn't at all surprised when the ruse worked, and the boy left his hiding place.

"I'm here, Nanny." Sam ran up to tuck his hand inside that of his caretaker, proving he could be manipulated through his kind heart.

"Come along then, laddie. Mrs. Pratt is serving our snack and then it's naptime for you."

While his nanny spoke, Sam smiled and waved to Mrs. Dorn, who was beaming and waving back, a silly grin splitting her face from ear to ear. Before the other two could leave the room, she said, "Grace, I've a small gift for Sammy here in me bag. Could he join us so I might give it to him?"

Nonplussed, Grace looked from one woman to the other. The silence grew until Sam broke it by running to Grace and pleading, "Please, Mummy, can I come back and visit with Mrs. Dorn after tea? I'm not at all tired and I hate napping." His voice rang with disgust when he spoke the last word. "Only babies have to nap and I'm a big boy. Please?"

"Now, Samuel." Mrs. Grieve interrupted his pleading. "Naptime is a rule. It's important to get some rest during the day in order to be awake for when your father comes home. Come along now."

A push from Henrietta forced Grace to step forward. "Nanny, would it be alright for Sammy to join us for a short while? Mrs. Dorn has come to visit especially to see him and has been thoughtful enough to bring a gift. I—I'd very much like it if he might have a few minutes with her."

All eyes rested on Flora who sighed and answered. "Very well, if you insist. I'll send him in for a few minutes after he eats, but we must stick to his routine as much as possible."

Grace heard the woman's frustration and she caught the look of exhaustion the other couldn't hide, then it dawned on her. It wasn't so much Sam who needed the nap, but his nanny.

Gently, she answered. "I'd appreciate it very much, Nanny. We won't keep him long."

As soon as the door closed behind the two, Mrs. Dorn blew her gasket and in true Henrietta style she proclaimed, "That woman puckers me bum. Let me tell ya, I've knots in me knickers from holding back the words on the tip of me tongue."

"Henrietta, behave!" Grace couldn't hide the giggle that broke loose. Biting down on her lower lip hadn't stopped it from emerging, and neither had swallowing repeatedly.

"Her majesty's got the sourest puss I've ever seen. Poor Sammy having to spend his days with the ole—"

Grace interrupted her tirade. "And I thought she looked very tired, the poor dear. Four-years-olds are a handful and Flora must be in her seventies. It can't be easy looking after a boy so lively."

"Poor dear—bah! Trust you to stick up for her. She's the reason you're lonely. If you could spend the day with

Sammy, you'd have more than enough to keep you busy."
A sniff lent her words the emphasis she intended.

"Don't you think she's done a good job with her charge?
I think Sam is wonderfully behaved." Grace knew that she
had to use her wiles to get Mrs. Dorn to see the vital hitch
in her argument.

"Why, he's a pet, he is. A lovely boy... Oh, yer a right
proper brat. You've tricked me."

Grace could almost see the wheels turning in the other's
head. Finally, her wait was rewarded.

"I suppose yer right. The spiteful cow has done a fairly
good job, but I think it's time she was put to pasture."

Just then Mrs. Platt arrived with a tea tray and Grace had
Mrs. Dorn help her organize their snack to take her mind
off her snit. She watched as the big-hearted woman set
aside a cookie—no doubt for when Sam returned, which
happened a short time later. He must have swallowed his
tea whole to have finished so quickly.

With peanut butter dotting his chin, Sam's innocent
rejoinder had everyone's ears perk up. "This is fun.
Usually I'm not allowed to have tea with Mummy. Nanny
says we mustn't bother her, that she needs her time for
herself." His inquiring gaze lifted to Grace, his green
dazzlers opened wide, questioning. "Why do you want to
be alone? Don't you like having tea with us?"

"Of course I do." The words burst out before she could
stop them. "Sammy-son, I love being with you—anytime. I
get lonely by myself. It's – it's boring!"

Chapter 23

Lucas stopped behind the open door, out of sight of the tea partiers, and listened to his wife speak. Her words reverberated: "It's boring!"

How often had those same words been thrown at him, spat in a voice full of disgust and unhappiness? *I'm bored.*

Some days he'd hated coming home and wouldn't have, except that a little boy had waited for him every night, a smile creasing up his chubby cheeks the minute his father had walked into the room.

Of course, then, Vanessa had spent as little time with Sammy as possible. From the day Flora had started working for them, she'd had strict instructions not to leave the boy with Vanessa. And those orders hadn't been issued by him, but by the boy's own mother. When he and Sam appeared together, she'd leave the room. In fact, most days, according to the housekeeper, she'd either kept to her room, worked ridiculous long hours in her studio or left the house.

In the last couple of years, she'd taken to leaving the house in the evenings, before he'd returned from work.

He'd gotten the feeling it was because Sam was staying up later and she hadn't wanted to be around the child. Then again, maybe it had been because she hadn't wanted to be around her husband?

He'd married a strange woman, no doubt about it. Turned out that everyone who'd assured him that she'd change after the boy's birth had been wrong. Dead wrong! She never had taken to her son. In fact, she hadn't let him near her. If Sam ran into her during the day, she'd freak if he weren't under his nanny's supervision.

Certainly, life in his home hadn't been a fairytale. More like a horror story, if the truth were known. The only place where they'd kept up some semblance of normality was their sex life.

She'd clung to him after she'd gotten her figure back. It hadn't taken her long, because she hadn't put on the extra weight so many other women did when pregnant. The doctor had been pleased with her control and, surprisingly, she'd had an easy time during the birth.

After six weeks, she'd come to him as if trying to make up for her rotten behavior. As long as he hadn't talked about Sam, they'd almost captured some of their earlier desire. He'd played the game, pretending everything was normal. But he'd never been able to feel the old enthusiasm for her or her lovely body. And she knew it. But how could a man be expected to make passionate love to the woman who so evidently hated his son—her son?

Not being a fool, it soon became clear to her that he'd changed. It was around that time she'd started disappearing in the evenings, returning later and later, stinking with booze, anger sizzling and barely controlled. After the first few times he'd questioned her, only to have her fly off the deep end, blaming him for all their troubles, he'd learned to shut up and look the other way.

Sam's giggles caught his attention and pulled him out of the funk that hovered, waiting to sink him with its claws of rotten memories. He stepped into the room in time to see Vanessa tickle Sam to stop him from getting the last cookie. She quickly passed the plate to Mrs. Dorn, and with her hand holding Sam back against the sofa, she laughed and said, "You must eat this, Henrietta. Sam will be too full to eat all his supper tonight."

Mrs. Dorn jokingly lifted the cookie to her mouth as if she were going to take a bite, "I did notice the young whippersnapper is getting a mite chubby. Maybe I should and save him from—"

Sam cut in, laughing gleefully, "I'm too thin to be chubby. And I'll be good and eat all my supper, really I will." Just then Sam spotted his father and, as usual, his face lit up and made Lucas's heart swell. He'd never get over the feeling that swamped him whenever he saw the adoration shining in his son's eyes.

"Daddy! You're home."

Lucas leaned down in time to catch the body flung at him with all the confidence of a little one who knew instinctively he'd never be dropped.

"Mummy! Daddy's home."

Lucas felt another chunk of granite around his heart crumble from words that made that organ sing.

"Yes, I can see that, Sammy-son. Would you like to go and tell Mrs. Pratt that your father's here and we'll need a fresh pot of tea?"

"I'll come with you," Mrs. Dorn stated. "If it's all right with you, Vanessa, I'm dying to see around the house. Could Sammy take me on a tour?"

"Of course, Mrs. Dorn." Lucas spoke before Vanessa

had the chance. "I'm home early today to work in my office here, so don't let me interrupt whatever you ladies had planned. I'll steal a quick cup of your tea and be out of your way."

"I'll take you around, Henrietta." Vanessa seemed insistent.

"No, luv, I'll be fine with my man, Sam. Stay and keep your husband company. You might have something you need to tell him." Mrs. Dorn's arched eyebrow spoke as plain as if she'd said the words aloud: *You need to talk!*

The adoring subject holding the hand of the little prince—with him talking a mile a minute—left the room. Vanessa, perched on the edge of the sofa across from Lucas, looked uneasy. She rubbed and squeezed her arms indicating nervousness, a new habit he'd never noticed before. He decided to put her out of her misery.

"You have something you want to tell me?" He mixed sugar into his tea but didn't trust himself to pick up the cup. For some strange reason, his hands were suddenly shaky, and he felt his bile begin to churn. Was she going to leave him? Her face wore a serious expression and she hadn't looked directly at him since the others had left the room.

He studied her face and then noticed her simple makeup and her choice of outfits—comfortably attractive but rather plain. Previously, whenever he and Vanessa were in this room, she'd look as if she'd just stepped out of a fashion magazine. Her clothes, expensive and classy, had been nonetheless extravagant. Liking dramatic effects, she'd dressed with verve and sometimes outlandish choices: fancy belts and scarves, lots of jewelry and loads of color that had often been hard on the eyes.

He liked the new look better. More approachable, and it

suited her new manner. Finally, she cleared her voice and leaned forward. The seriousness that lit her face literally scared the bejesus out of him.

Maybe he didn't want to hear what she had to say after all? And before he knew he would, he uttered those very words. "Do I want to hear this?" How pathetic could a man get? Angry with himself, he crossed his arms and slouched back against the cushion. He knew his attitude reeked of cowardice, but he didn't care. Finally, when he thought they just might have a chance, she was going to break his heart once again, his and Sam's. He didn't know if he could take any more.

"I want to be a nurse." Once the words were said, she lifted her face and stared him straight in the eye—earnest, genuine.

Feeling like a daft prick didn't sit well with him, but he deserved the title. Why did he still insist on thinking the worst? Being realistic, he knew it was because of her past behavior. *But recently...?*

It took a minute before his stomach landed back in place. He looked at her, looked deep into her sincere eyes and saw the fear of being dismissed that she couldn't hide. *So different from the old days when she'd shown no emotions.* The change still mystified him.

"What did you say?" He had to be sure.

She repeated it, her voice shaky. "I-I want to be a nurse." She was determined. He knew it in his gut. She meant it, and he'd better take her seriously or he'd be in for it. After all, he'd seen her temper tantrums and they weren't a pretty sight. As big and strong as he was, many a time she'd made him sit up and take notice and wish he could tuck his tail and slink away.

Ruddy hell! Stop thinking about what she used to be like.

"A nurse!? What about your art? You have—ah—had a wonderful career. Do you want to give that up to go to nursing school?" Shocked astonishment rang in his voice, even after he'd admonished himself to be careful.

"Yes, I do." Once she'd made the statement, he noticed how calm she sounded. A kind of serenity had taken hold, and by her relaxed stance, he could see that she had every intention of either getting his approval or bypassing him and going ahead anyway. That stubborn chin was angled in just the way he'd seen hundreds of times.

"And if I don't agree?" *Bloody flaming hell!* Why did he have to always push? How did those words break free from his normal restraints? Now he was in for it.

She sighed, straightened her shoulders and put her hands together as if in prayer. "I really hope you will, Lucas. Look, let me try to explain. All the time I spent in the hospital, frightened and in pain, the nurses looked after me. They helped me get back my strength and took away the fear and the loneliness. I want to do the same, help others. I know it'll be a long road, but I'm in no hurry. I can enroll in the nursing classes at the hospital, and Lucas, I promise not to let it interfere with my responsibilities here at home." She moved to sit next to him and tentatively reached out to touch his knee. Her earnestness brought a lump to his throat. *How could this sweetheart be the same woman who he'd hated so much?*

"Please think about it, Lucas. I'd never go without your consent, but it means ever so much to me."

Without another word, he scooped her onto his knee and into his arms and rocked her from side to side. He even patted her back like he did to Sam when he needed to be soothed. "Darling, you can do whatever you wish. If it'll make you happy to take up nursing, then that's what you must do. We'll make it happen, never worry."

She buried her face into his neck and her whisper tickled his ear. "Oh, Lucas, how wonderful! I'm so happy." With her arms wrapped tightly around his back, she rocked with him. Her breasts flattened against his chest and pleasure exploded as if he were boiling oil and she were drops of cold water.

Like a brash teen with no control, ardor stormed his body, which hardened instantly, and turned his brain to pure mush. He searched for her lips and the minute he tasted her sweetness, he became lost.

At first, she seemed to hesitate, but he wouldn't allow her any choice. Insistence paid off and soon she moaned, becoming a willing victim in his arms. Her mouth opened, and he invaded, searching for her tongue to lick and suck like he knew she enjoyed.

Unlike the last time he'd made love to her on this very sofa, she seemed to be more comfortable with his advances. He felt her hands in his hair, caressing. With desire smoldering, she returned his kisses and arched into him, which brought every part of her body into closer contact, close enough for him to search under her sweater in order to crush her breasts in his hands. Touch them in ways he knew she liked. Brush her nipples with his thumbs, sculpting them, loving the softness of her skin and the plumpness filling his hands. Lucas knew he was getting close to making love to her right there in a room open to anyone. He had to stop, but how? She was too damn sweet.

Too intoxicating.

Too willing.

Finally, he wrenched himself back and held her swaying toward him. Her lips were plump from his kisses, lipstick smudged. The green in her eyes were huge pools of emerald wildness. And the ultimate weapon, her beautiful hair, which was messed by his hands and floating around her lovely face, turned him on once again.

Just as he leaned in to scoop her back into his arms, all control lost, she pushed him away, straightened and turned to the doorway. He heard the voices approaching also and took the next few seconds to straighten his clothing, cross his legs and whisper. "Tonight, darling, we'll be together. And you can do the one thing that pleases you above all else. I'll come for you—tonight."

Chapter 24

For the rest of the afternoon and evening, Grace floated between heaven and insanity. Mrs. Dorn's sharp eyes noticed that something had happened. But they never got time alone for Grace to ask her advice. Besides, she wasn't sure if it was something she wanted to discuss with anyone else. On the other hand, what in the world would happen when Lucas realized she had no idea what he'd meant by her doing the one thing she loved?

By the time she heard the knock on her bedroom door that night, she'd worked herself into such a state, she all but passed out. Whether it was because of the hysteria going on inside her imagination from a fear of failure, or because she was losing her mind, it wasn't clear. But she'd begun to worry that she was hearing voices and it had taken all her willpower and concentration to shut them down. Swallowing, she once again fluffed her hair, squared her shoulders and opened the door.

Lucas stood with a bottle of wine in one hand and two fluted glasses in the other. He arranged them on the small round table by the window and turned to gaze at her adoringly. His flannel pajama bottoms hung loose and long, covering his toes. And a sleeveless white undershirt hid part of his chest, but not all. For the first time, Grace marveled that a man who worked as an architect would be in such great shape. The muscles in his arms and back looked well-honed. Teased by the pleasure surging through her, she stifled a whimper.

"Would you like a glass of wine?" His raspy voice activated her hunger and rather than letting him see her stuttering like a schoolgirl, she nodded. He poured them each a glass and carried them over to where she stood rooted to the floor.

"To new beginnings." He passed over her drink and held his glass up to clink against hers as a toast. He took a sip, then stared at her from her feet to her face. Huskiness obscuring his usual calm tones, he said, "You look beautiful."

Considering it had taken her an hour just to choose which nightgown to wear, fearing none of them were 'her', she swallowed and nodded her thanks. She'd finally found one still with a price tag affixed that suited. The white had made her hesitate, but then she'd shrugged and thought the color rather appropriate. It was the softness of the thick cotton and the lack of sexy styling that made her put it on. Only after she looked in the mirror, did she realize the garment projected quaint and lovely—and virginal. Then his knock on the door had robbed her of making a new choice.

A buzzing sounded in her head and she took a huge gulp of wine hoping to deaden the noise. She felt lightheaded. Knowing the wine hadn't had enough time to work, she wished she'd taken an aspirin. Nerves would account for the trauma, which in turn would account for the headache, but it was the weird whispers that really irritated. The second gulp of wine went down smoother and before she knew it, she held an empty glass.

Lucas watched her, smiling. "You're nervous."

Words erupted, and Grace couldn't stop them. "I don't remember. I'm sorry but I don't remember anything." His threat of sending her away if she didn't perform as before had haunted her. The words had played over and over until she felt as if she were a bit mad. "I don't think I can do this."

He smiled tenderly. "Yes, you can."

"I need more time."

"There is no more time. We're fighting for our marriage here, and we need to know if it can be saved."

"What if it can't?"

"Then you leave."

Heavens! He meant it. She could see how serious he was. "What about Sammy?"

"It would be best to make a clean break. I could never trust you alone with him after what happened."

Again, he hinted at something horrible she'd done to their son. *Oh God, what had that woman done that she had to live down?*

"Look, I didn't come here to fight, Vanessa. I came to give you and our marriage another chance. You've changed, and I like it. I like you. Maybe it's enough to start with?"

"I like you too." It was the truth and easy to admit.

"Come here, darling. Come to me. I promise to take things slow. And if you're uncomfortable, we'll stop. All right?"

She stepped forward, and childishly her left hand rose to her cheek while the right one handed him her empty glass, which he put along with his full one back on the table.

"Did you know that since the crash you hold your cheek, especially in moments of stress? I don't recall there being any specific injuries there and I don't remember you having that particular habit before the accident." With his head held sideways, he waited.

Stunned, thrown off-kilter, she didn't know what to say. "I-I didn't know I did it all the time. I'm sorry."

"Why be sorry. It's kind of endearing." He smiled and took off his shirt, then stepped back in front of her once again.

Covering the middle of his chest was a glorious sweep of springy dark hair, defining his muscular frame. This captured her interest and it was all she could do to keep her fingers from playing with the rioting curls. Seconds passed, and finally he lifted the long hair framing her shoulders and pushed it toward her back. "I miss brushing your hair."

Huskiness made his voice low and the sound worked like surges of seduction that tickled along her nerves. Her mouth felt dry. She licked her lips and watched as his glittering eyes followed her tongue.

Before she realized his intentions, he leaned forward and licked them also. His breath, hot on her face, seemed erotic and sensations blasted all over her body. Her breasts tightened, engorged. Wetness surged, forcing her muscles to clench. Her sensitive skin pebbled, sending messages of delight from her brain to every cell in her body. Only his touch soothed her panic.

With a small cry, she lunged herself into his waiting arms. He lifted her and carried her over to the side of the bed, where he set her on her feet in front of him.

Holding her close, he kissed her deeply. His moans added to the moment, affecting her until she could drown in his tenderness. Soon, he'd worked her nightgown slowly up her body, until forced to back away, he waited for her to lift her arms so he could take it off completely.

Naked, shyness forced her close to him again, and this time she felt his hardened desire nudging against her bare stomach and she swooned. If he hadn't been so perceptive, she might have fallen, because there was no strength at all left in her rubbery legs.

"And you were worried. You know that this has always been the best part of our relationship. I've always wanted you, Van. Even when I was angry, you could always turn me on." His kisses had moved to her shoulder, forcing her head back to give him access to her neck.

Muddled, overcome with desire, words broke free. "Don't call me that."

"I never knew why you hated that name, darling girl. But I'll call you anything that makes you happy."

"Then call me darling." This time she took control and kissed him for the first time. Putting all her emotions into it, she rubbed her breasts against his chest, her hardened nipples trailed through the soft hair. Instinctively, she knew he'd be pleased.

"Darling," he groaned. "My beautiful darling." He lifted her until her legs straddled his hips and he pushed his manhood against the portal that screamed for him. Except he was still clothed.

Only for a moment. Strong enough to balance her by leaning against the bed, he yanked at his bottoms and wiggled until they dropped to pool by his feet. Let loose, his manhood sprang to life and tickled at the entrance to ecstasy.

"Lucas." Grace whispered his name, begging for him to do something. A fire had begun in her body and the flames were destroying every vestige of shyness. His body, wrapped in her arms, became the pinnacle of her existence. She needed him to make her truly a woman. She wanted him to teach her the delights of sex. And she desired his body like nothing else she'd ever known.

He lowered her to the bed, landed on top of her, then rolled to the side. Both were naked, both breathing hard. He leaned away as if waiting for her to make the next move. Hesitating, she stared into his half-lidded eyes. Without understanding why it seemed so important, she put her hands on his chest and stroked from his shoulders to his stomach. Delighted with his body, she wondered if a man needed a woman's affirmation as much as a woman needed her man's?

As if she'd passed a test of some sort, he gathered her close, rolled over her and kissed her until she felt like every star in the universe sparkled behind her eyelids. There was little breath left by the time his lips moved to her breasts. He licked and nuzzled all the while his hands stroked and caressed.

Other places screamed for his attention and she brazenly wriggled under him, opening her legs, hoping to capture that which prodded.

"Don't," Lucas groaned. "It's been too long. I'll never last."

"I'm sorry. You feel so good, I can't help it."

She felt him grin by the way his whiskers tickled her skin. "You always were in a hurry to reach the end instead of enjoying the buildup."

Like cold water, his words struck her, and something shriveled inside then disappeared. Emptiness filled the gap. It was the strangest thing she'd ever known. But, in some way, it was as if she was whole again, on her own and alone with Lucas.

She lowered her legs, gently caressed his head and sighed. Whatever he had in mind would be fine with her. No longer did she feel that burning need to reach orgasm. Instead all she cared about was to show the man in her bed how much he pleased her.

Experiencing every touch of his hands, every kiss, soon she felt sensitized urges build that carried her along blissfully. Like a skilled musician, he played her, and the seductive music they made together lifted her to dizzying heights. Muscles she didn't know existed began to clamor and spasm, her drenched orifice which he played with lovingly for long moments screamed with delight and her heart filled with adoration. This man made her soul smile.

Never had she felt so happy, and when he entered her she welcomed him with kisses, cries and a satisfying sigh.

They sang together, moan for moan, whimpers from her and his groans in answer. Moving in unison, he loved her gently, slowly, deeply until overcome. Then his thrusts took on the momentum of an aggressor. She loved every minute and accommodated his deeper penetrations. Consumed, she tried to show him how affected she was by his loving. Her body felt like heated fluid, and hot wildness was her response. Never had she lacked restraint and she couldn't care less. All she wanted to do was prove to this man how much she loved him.

It was the last thought she had when an indescribable release swept over her, caught her up and carried her along. Strong contractions gave her great satisfaction, held him in place and obviously added to his delight. Within moments he groaned expressively, and she felt his own release pumping into her.

If her subconscious could record this experience, paste it in her memory and keep it forever, she would, and happily. She never wanted to let go of how she felt right now, at this exact moment. Never, ever forget it.

"Good Lord, Vanessa, that was incredible. Different, but the best yet."

His words shouldn't have pleased her, but they did. In her conscious mind, she glowed and smiled. But, at the same time, she felt a sadness gathering, escalating, and had no idea why these two emotions were combating each other.

He kissed her one last time and then turned them both so they lay side by side. Then he said. "I'm ready; you can go ahead and play. In fact, you can do whatever you want to me and I'll be your willing slave."

Fear made her tremble and ache. Blank, her mind was totally, sickeningly blank. She had no idea what he wanted her to do. No idea at all.

Chapter 25

"Run your fingers through the hair on his chest." The voice sounded grating and desperate.

Even though his arms held her tightly, she reacted like she'd seen a ghost. Only in her case, she'd heard it.

"What's wrong darling? You've stiffened right up? Is everything okay?"

She leaned back, forcing him to loosen his arms, and said. "Did you hear someone speak?"

"Don't be an idiot. He can't hear me. Just do what I told you, and he won't send us away."

"There's no one here but you and me, darling. And...we've just had the best sex ever."

Before she could stop herself, the words popped out. "I-I prefer to think of it as making love." As soon as she heard what she'd stammered, shyness had her groaning, closing her eyes and seeking his warmth.

"Those are my words, darling. But you've always played down the emotional aspect and called it what it was—to your way of thinking—having sex."

"Well, I've changed my mind." Needing to hide, her face

nestled close to his body and the chest hairs tickled her cheek. Automatically, she ran her fingers through them to smooth them away.

He moaned.

"*Keep it up! This is what he's been expecting. Play with the hairs and curl them around you fingers. Even rub your face over his chest and kiss him there. Do it!*"

Grace anticipated the voice this time and wasn't as shocked. *Vanessa?*

"*Yes, I'll go and leave you alone. But promise me you'll make him believe you're me. He can't send us away. Promise me, or I'll make you sorry.*" This time Vanessa used a tone that brooked no denial. Clearly the spirit had taken charge.

Lucas's voice broke into her inner discussion. "I've missed you petting me. I never knew why you were so enamored with the hair on my chest, but since it's the only time when I've known you to act so affectionately, I find it rather endearing."

As Grace followed orders, a peaceful sensation flowed over her and a sigh escaped. The hairs were soft and brushed her face in a nice way. She kissed him and nuzzled his chest, and all the while she knew that her invader—actually, no... *she* was the invader—had taken over, carrying on in her stead.

Stunned by her realization of who was the victim and who was the villain had weakened her barriers. The guilt of another forcing her movements at such a personal moment clamored in her consciousness. But she had no defense. This was, after all, Vanessa's body.

Even though she wasn't directing the playful petting, she'd benefitted from his reactions. He hugged her close, kissed her forehead and covered them with the fallen quilt.

"Sleep now, my love. In the morning, we'll talk. I never thought I'd say this, Vanessa, but I'm glad you're home."

One last kiss and he turned so her head lay on his shoulder, while the warmth of his hand caressed the skin on her arm and lulled her anxieties.

Grace siphoned through her inner self and realized she was completely alone. That the voice had quieted, and the presence was gone.

Magic, exactly like she'd envisioned when it had happened to another, had now taken over her life.

She'd remembered the many discussions with Dani, Dr. Andrews' niece, who'd been on a similar adventure. She'd taken up residence inside the body of a young American reporter, had fallen in love with him and still waited for the day to be reacquainted. Her description of body-sharing had sounded like fun. But for Grace, it hadn't felt good at all. Horrifying or scary explained it much better.

What was she to do? Returning to her body wasn't an option. Was she to be locked inside with Vanessa forever?

Oh, God! She couldn't bear it!

Chapter 26

The next morning, Lucas's kisses woke her from bad dreams—dreams where she'd been jailed. And the bars had closed in on her so she couldn't move more than a few inches in either direction. Glad to be awake, she thought to push him away and get out of the bed.

But his lips were warm and searching. And she was scared and worried. Before she could find the strength for control, his wandering hands began fondling her breasts and his kisses were travelling from her neck and under her ears, where there seemed to be a particularly sensitive path downwards to her waiting nipples. How could something that felt so ruddy good be wrong?

Lost, she let him lead her wherever he wanted. And he led her straight to heaven. By the time their breathing had slowed and they lay entwined, arms wrapped around each other, legs tangled, she realized that there had only been two people in the bed—her and Lucas. A sigh of relief escaped.

"I could stay here like this all day. You make me feel like I'm a young stud again." The smile in his voice lightened her heart.

"Me, too." *And the truth shall set you free!* Right. Now, where did that come from? Obviously from her own guilt because they were still alone.

He kissed her again, his lips crushing hers. "Tell me to stop." Good Lord, his raspy voice could be used for sex commercials. Whatever the product, women would flock to buy.

She caught his gaze; grey eyes sultry with desire stared into hers, and she couldn't look away. "Don't look at me. I'm weak—honestly, no self-discipline whatsoever."

He grinned, kissed her forehead and rubbed his whiskered chin over her nose. "And I've always thought you were the strong one in the family. Goes to show what I know." Teasing, he smiled, and she smiled back.

"Okay. I shall be the boss of this party and call the shots. You, madam, will get your lovely little derriere out of my bed, have a super day and return here tonight to carry on where we left off. Do I make myself clear?" He pointed his finger at her first, and then waved it toward the room as if he could magically remove her from the bed.

"Nay, sir, I'm afraid you speak falsely. You must remove your lovely... ah...bum from *my* bed, have a super day and return tonight if you so desire." She followed his hand movements exactly and watched as surprised pleasure lit his face.

"Darling, I love it when you're playful. Let's stay like this forever. Don't change, don't be unhappy ever again." The earnest tone in his voice and in his gaze revealed the importance of his words. Uttered as a slightly tortured request, she knew that even an idiot couldn't ignore the emphatic plea.

As if he'd overstepped boundaries, he kissed her gently,

stood and gathered his clothes. Then butt naked and whistling, he sauntered to a door on the far side. She realized he could reach his own room through a passageway connecting his to hers. She'd snuck a peek around the space when she'd first arrived, but shyness had stopped her from exploring further. A plan to open the door and leave it that way settled into her head and she wondered if she had the nerve.

Gathering her blanket to cover her nakedness, she closed her eyes and let the impression of his naked body return. Tall, not just in height, but from the way he carried himself, lithe from workouts or maybe from nature, he was every woman's dream of a seducer. If she never got to spend another night with him, at least she'd have this memory to cherish. *Stop thinking like the old Grace! Be positive!*

She lay back against the pillows and threaded her fingers through her hair, a habit she'd found soothing lately. As if it had a mind of its own, her hand snaked to her left cheek and she quickly forced it into her lap where she folded it with the other to stop their shaking.

Stop putting it off. Sooner or later, you have to deal with what's happened. Hating to accept the shared occupancy of her new body, she had no choice. Though it was grinding down the precious memory of the night before, she couldn't pretend it hadn't happened.

Vanessa? Her instincts warned her she was alone, but she had to try.

Nothing!

"Can we speak together, please?"

Still nothing.

No matter how long she was ignored, it looked like Vanessa had the power to return whenever she wanted.

Grace needed to accept that she now faced a terrible dilemma. And she couldn't possibly do so alone. A picture of her best friends entered her thoughts and she felt better instantly. She knew exactly who could help her make sense of this situation.

Chapter 27

Grace banged the brass knocker on the front door of Dr. Andrews' ivy-covered house and waited for Henrietta or Tobias to answer. She noticed the devil's grinning image on the fancy hardware in front of her and shivered. An omen, she wondered? Then shook off her misgivings and lifted it once more.

"Aye there, hang on." Mrs. Dorn sounded miffed. Probably she had been upstairs cleaning and climbing up and down wasn't easy nowadays. "Hold yer horses," she bellowed.

The door swung open. Mrs. Dorn wearing a pink housedress decorated with frills from under her chin to the top of her apron let out a shriek of gladness upon spying her visitor. "Gr... blasted hell! I mean, Vanessa, dearie, you're a sight for sore eyes. Forgive me child, I've been so scatty lately, I've forgotten that you were coming to visit." Her plump fingers worked at tidying her hair, which only knocked the flowered kerchief, wrapped around her curlers, over her ear at an endearing, lopsided angle.

A giggle escaped before Grace could stop herself, and then her bottom lip began to wiggle, and she sniffed. "Actually, this is an impromptu visit, Henrietta. Is Tobias here? I'm in terrible trouble and I need h-help." The last word ended in a sob.

Warm arms encircled her, and she was cuddled in affection. "Well, stone the crows, child, he's in his office. We'll go right there and whatever is botherin' ya, poor soul, will be all fixed in a jiffy. Come along 'ere now."

Tobias jumped up at the sight of the two women and rushed around his messy office to help guide Grace to the visitor's chair in front of his desk. He patted her shoulders at the same time as giving directions to his employee. "Mrs. Dorn, could you make us a cup of tea. I think Grace needs the comfort."

"Doctor! Her name is *Vanessa*, as you've warned me repeatedly, and I might add, rather rudely at times. And don't be so daft in thinking I'll be leaving our lass at a time like this. The tea can wait."

Dr. Andrews shot a raised eyebrow and a disgruntled glare toward his housekeeper, who sniffed and turned to Grace. "Now, lovie, go on and tell us what's got you so upset. There, there."

"I believe my patient wishes a word with me in private, Mrs. *Dorn*." The doctor pointed to the door with a no-nonsense attitude, expecting to be obeyed.

Grace held on to Mrs. Dorn's hand and, in her misery, she did something she'd never done before. She overrode a doctor's order. "Please, Tobias. Let Henrietta stay. I need both of you to help me sort out this nightmare. I guess I should have expected something like this to happen, but I didn't." She had to stop and swallow the wail building inside. She gritted her teeth and blinked before she trusted her voice again. "Now I'm in a terrible dilemma, and I have no idea what to do."

"I would venture to disagree... Oh, fine! Who am I to ignore your request? After all, I'm just the doctor here. If you wish to get a *second opinion* with the likes of Mrs. Dorn, so be it." A stuffy note entered his tone and Grace felt the darkness within her lighten. "But ladies, *I* need a cuppa and so I insist that we resume this discussion in the kitchen, where Mrs. Dorn will do the work she's abundantly paid for and provide us with tea."

Soon, they were in a cheerful room warmed by the fireplace where Mrs. Dorn's cozy rocker sat, surrounded by baskets brim-filled with multicolored wools.

Quickly, Mrs. Dorn poured boiling water from the copper kettle that miraculously appeared to be ready at a moment's notice. While she scurried around her domain, the china teapot was left to steep. The wooden table highlighted by a hand-made crocheted doily was quickly laden with dainties and eventually cups of fragrant tea.

Dr. Andrews cut into the filler discussion about how much rain had fallen and steered the conversation back to Grace's problem.

Feeling much more composed, Grace began the explanation of what had occurred the night before. "Lucas and I were... ah... in bed... ah... We were... ah—"

Mrs. Dorn's sigh was comical. "Hopefully, you was getting it on, Gracie. Surely to goodness, there's no shame between a husband and wife doing what comes naturally. In fact, isn't that what we'd planned on when this switch began?"

"Yes, Henrietta, but I only ever *planned* on there being two of us in the bed. Not three!"

"Blimey, now that's a bit of a sticky wicket. What say

you, Doctor?"

Dr. Andrews answered without any doubt at all. "Vanessa's returned."

Grace nodded. "I'm sure of it. You see, there was one thing Vanessa did to Lucas when they were... ah... intimate. Earlier in the day, he'd warned me that if I didn't remember what it was, he'd never believe I was really his Vanessa and that I would need to leave."

"Goodness me, what did you do?" Mrs. Dorn sat so far forward in her chair, Grace worried the woman might topple over.

"That's enough, Mrs. Dorn." Dr. Andrews's firm tone brooked no argument. "I'll be asking the questions." Tobias reached over to take Grace's hand in his. In a warmer tone, he asked. "What did you do?"

The loud snort from Mrs. Dorn eased Grace's stress, as did the stiffening of Tobias's shoulders and the rolling of his eyes. She smiled and answered them both. "I prayed. I had no idea what he was talking about. But one thing led to another and, I must say, our joining was miraculous. Then Lucas obviously expected me to perform in some sort of way that Vanessa always did, and I couldn't." Her eyes filled. "Not until she instructed me to stroke his chest."

"Therefore, she helped you." Tobias was all doctor now. His manner reminded her of the same one he'd used numerous times with other patients while she'd assisted as his nurse. Even Henrietta sat back, knowing her place.

"Helped me? Maybe. But at the same time, she threatened. Her words were more like—do as I say, or I'll make you sorry. It was extreme and frightening."

"Has she been in contact with you again?"

"No. I've pleaded with her continuously to come out so

we could talk, but she's refusing to acknowledge me at all. Tobias, it's very strange. It's like I know she's there. I can sense her spirit hovering in the background, but there's no response."

"It's your imagination, Gr... dear. It's because you know she's inside that you feel this way. If Vanessa was active at all, you'd have no doubts. When Doctor Norman and I performed our intensive study on this phenomenon, we came to realize that each of the souls has the ability to open themselves or close down completely. But we could never fool each other. If we tried to lurk in the background, the other always knew. And I have no doubt it's the same for you and Vanessa. If she's left any of her lines opened, you'll know."

"Then I have no idea why she's hiding. For whatever reason, the poor dear doesn't want to acknowledge me."

Mrs. Dorn, chin between her thumb and forefinger, interrupted as if musing out loud. "Doctor, if'n it's like you said, that in the hospital Vanessa wanted to die, I'm wondering if she feels angry with Grace for keeping her alive?"

Shocked, Grace looked from one to the other occupants at the table. "What do you mean she *wanted* to die?"

First, Tobias glared at Mrs. Dorn and then he cleared his throat. "I did tell you they thought she'd tried to commit suicide."

"Yes... you did, didn't you? But no one knew for sure. It was a supposition because of her not leaving any skid marks on the road."

"Yes, well, they may have been correct. The rest of the doctors working her case were confounded as to why she hadn't improved. Strange as it may seem, we all felt that the woman had... well... willed herself to pass on. That she'd given up, and no matter what we did, she wouldn't improve. The surgery she'd undergone had been brilliantly performed. We could find no physical reason for her to fade the way she did."

"Good heavens! What you're saying is that by me possessing her body and infusing my will, forcing her to recover, we took away her undeniable right to leave this world."

Mrs. Dorn snorted rather loudly. "Oh, piffle! Such rubbish! The woman was a flaming nutcase and you, my love, must take very good care of that perfectly lovely body. If she tries to give you any nonsense, you fight the chit off. Right, Doctor?"

"Either that or bring her to me so I may reach her. Whatever you do, don't let Lucas know what has happened. He wouldn't understand."

Chapter 28

"I don't understand?" Lucas looked at her across the breakfast table. "What's your big hurry? You've only just gotten out of the hospital and you want to start studying nursing next month?"

Grace had known he'd demand an explanation, and she had one prepared. "It's not that I want to, as much as the classes begin at the hospital then, and I don't wish to wait until the next opening. Lucas, you must understand, I need an occupation."

Lucas went to her seat, lifted her from the chair so he could sit himself and gathered her onto his knee. He held her close and nuzzled her neck. "I wasn't going to say anything just yet, at least until I had everything sorted. It's meant to be a surprise. I'd hoped to persuade you to renew our wedding vows in front of our vicar, my family and our friends."

Surprised delight filled her, making her lean back and smile into his face. "My goodness, I never thought of such a thing." Little did the man know that actually being a bride was a pipe dream for a woman who had never expected to marry.

"Our first nuptials were so unadorned and basic: no church, no family, just two strangers in a registry office. I kind of liked the idea of us making it a real occasion—me in a tux and you in a long white gown, flowers, the whole nine yards. I can take care of all the arrangements so you needn't fuss. We'll make it for the end of the month, shall we? Your only chore will be to buy the perfect dress. And I know that your favorite shops should have whatever you need. Now, I suppose if you really insist on carrying through with your nursing plans, we won't be organizing a honeymoon."

"A long weekend in Paris would please me very well, just the two of us." Grace had never been to Paris. Knowing it was a city to delight lovers, she recognized that, for her, it would be like a dream come true.

"Now that, my dear betrothed wife, I can make happen." Pleasure lighting his face, Lucas kissed her. Adoration shone, illuminating his eyes with a look every woman desired to see on the face of the man she loved. "So, will you marry me?"

Filled with pleasure and reciprocating happiness, Grace beamed back her delight. "Yes, please. We could invite Tobias and Henrietta, your workmates, even the house staff. Most of all, think how pleased Sammy will be as your best man." His excitement had fueled hers. She couldn't contain her satisfaction at the thought of pledging herself to love and honor this wonderful man for the rest of her life.

"Goodness, I never thought of that. You're right, Vanessa. Sammy will be thrilled. God, I love you, darling. You've made me a very happy man today. In fact, I'm so drunk with joy that I completely forgot your dilemma.

You're still having some misery with your day to day life, not having enough to occupy your time?"

She nodded shyly.

Silence reigned for a few moments before he added. "Darling, are you quite sure that working with sick people all day will make you happy? You've never mentioned this whim before."

"Lucas, it isn't a whim. I do know exactly what I'm doing. Please trust me on this."

"Fine, I'll say no more on the subject. My only concern is that the nursing won't start for some weeks. According to you, we must fill in those days between now and then."

"If I could remember how to paint, I'd be out in my studio and you'd never question me filling those hours, would you?"

"You're right." Lucas caught her eyes and stared directly into her conscience. "Frankly, Vanessa, I find it preposterous that your amazing talent doesn't come naturally. Have you tried going out there to experiment? See if the knowledge is buried in your subconscious?" As he questioned, his eyes narrowed, and he wore a disbelieving frown.

Uncomfortable, Grace knew better than to look away. Yet it took all her willpower to sustain the connection. "No! I've not had the urge and, therefore, I haven't attempted it."

"Come with me now. It's a test that needs to happen. I'm certain you'll have retained the ability, and it'll just take you being amongst your painting paraphernalia for the urge to return."

Grace snatched her hand from him and held it to her stomach, hoping to hide the shivers of fear and the goose bumps of panic. "No! I don't want to."

"Darling, I must insist. I believe you're afraid for no reason, and that you will surprise yourself by still retaining the abilities you were born with. They were ingrained in you, darling. I have no doubt; it's why you were so successful. Come, trust me." He encircled her shoulders and began leading her in the direction of the small workshop that was connected to the house through a back hallway.

Everything inside her screamed 'No', and yet she could say nothing. Similarly, being led to a guillotine had probably felt the same to people in earlier centuries because life would soon be over for them. That's exactly how Grace felt. Once Lucas realized she had no talents whatsoever, he wouldn't believe her to be his true wife. He'd send her away and she would wither and want to die.

The large, bright room, windows on three sides, smelled precisely how one would expect where a person worked with oils, turpentine and paint thinners. There were canvasses stacked against one wall, some partially finished, others blank. On an easel in the middle of the room sat a timeworn, unframed portrait of a lovely young woman who looked to have lived in the eighteen hundreds. Her blue gown had greyed over the years and her face had been destroyed by age and, most likely, bad conditions.

What a shame! An emotional reaction flooded through Grace. Even though she had no talent as an artist, she loved works of art and appreciated their beauty.

"This was the commission you'd just consented to accept the day before the accident. And if I remember correctly, since I had been home when they delivered the parcel and passed it to you, by your positive reaction, I believe you were rather excited about the challenge. While you were in the hospital, I had numerous calls about you finishing this piece and had to explain that you were incapable of working. Your agent, Shawn Warner, insisted we leave the work here in case you were to recover. He claimed the owners wanted your special talent. That you were the only one who could do the job properly and it was the type of painting you most loved to work on."

"It's really quite sad, isn't it?" Grace walked toward the easel and reached her fingers toward the face of the woman. "Repaired, she would be beautiful again."

A force, from deep inside, burst into life and she felt taken over by the power of a mind much stronger than her own. Her hand picked up a tool she had no knowledge of and began to brush away particles near the edge of the frame. Having no idea of how or what she did, nonetheless, her hand seemed capable and her movements deft and deliberate.

Lucas moved to stand behind her. "There, darling. It's exactly what I expected. You can't help yourself. I'm relieved, Vanessa. You don't need to take on a whole new career, not when you can carry on with your old one."

Inside, Grace screamed silently. She struggled, wrestling for her future. She won. Throwing down the brush, she backed away from the painting, her hands held in front of her as if to ward off the devil. "No! I don't want to hide away in this dreary room any longer. I want to be in a place where I can help people. Lucas, the whole time I spent at the hospital, I watched how caring and kind the nurses were who gave me back my life, who washed and fed me and took such good care to see that I recovered. I want to do the same for others."

Lucas appeared shocked by her outburst. "Dearest, calm yourself! If that's what you want, then so be it. I shall certainly support your decision."

Grace turned her back to the man whose face held caring and sympathy—and extreme loving tenderness. Unexpected anger swelled inside, and her body became tense with the force of the overwhelming sensation. Swallowing the acid burning her insides, she soon realized she was in for the fight of her life.

Chapter 29

From that moment on, the days passed in a whirlwind. Grace signed up for her classes, gathered the multitude of textbooks and other school supplies she would need to become a student once again, and ran around the town with lists a mile long that she slowly ticked off.

Her coming wedding played a big part in her busyness and she loved explaining to others that she was to be remarried soon.

One day, she picked up Henrietta and they drove to one of the shops Vanessa had favored. The back section of the store held wedding garments and that's where they headed.

"Mrs. Knight. How delightful to see you again." A stick of a woman dressed in the latest fashion and wearing far too much makeup rushed to approach.

"Hello, Nancy." Thankful for the nametag worn by the clerk, Grace held out her hand and hid the smile created from the shocked appearance of the other woman. She'd obviously never received such kind treatment from Vanessa. "This is my friend, Henrietta Dorn."

"Jolly nice to meet you." Cheery as only Mrs. Dorn could be, she stuck out her own hand and waited for the limp shaking from the flummoxed lady.

Once the civilities were over, Nancy asked, "What can I help you with on this lovely day?"

Grace answered shyly. "We've come for a wedding dress. My husband is arranging for us to renew our vows and he wishes for me to have a formal white gown. We're to have all the guests we never invited the first time around. There'll even be a reception in the garden after the church ceremony."

Stunned, Nancy's eyes grew large as she stepped back. "Yes, of course, Mrs. Knight. How lovely. We have many frocks for you to choose from. If you'll follow me and sit over there, I'll pull out the ones I know you'll adore." She pointed to pink velvet chairs in the boutique where one other elderly customer sat fidgeting.

As they waited, Henrietta swiveled around in her chair, first to one side and then the other. "Blimey, pet, this is a flaming expensive place. Are you sure Lucas told you to come here?"

"Yes. See, he wrote it down." She showed Henrietta a slip of paper. "According to him, this is where Van... I bought most of my clothes."

Before Mrs. Dorn could reply, a young woman dressed as a bride entered the room to stand on the well-lit dais in front of huge mirrors. Turning this way and that, Grace could see the yearning delight shining on her face. She wore a gown of white satin studded with pearls and rhinestones, the skirt billowing out from her slightly plump waist. Every step she took, the delightful creation displayed her body in the best possible way. The form-fitting front and the stylish train followed her every move.

They watched as an older woman approached and listened to her hurtful words. "I don't like it, Carol. Take the other dress. And hurry, we haven't all day."

"But Mother, the puffy sleeves were horrid. And... and flappy. This dress is truly fashionable."

"It makes you look like a harlot. Take the other dress or go without."

Just in time, Grace pulled Henrietta back from making a fuss, as she was wont to do when faced with such meanness. Instead, she felt her own body brace, rage working as the stiffener. Unaccustomed in the past to voicing her opinion, other than on the wards, she nevertheless spoke up. With her tone pitched louder than usual, she said. "Carol, that dress is lovely. Is it not, Nancy? You could be a model of how every bride wants to appear on *her* day."

Nancy, bless her soul, stepped up and most likely lost a sale. "You look beautiful, dear."

Carol turned to face the three women. Silence lasted for quite a few moments. Everyone held their breath. And then she dropped her head and replied, "Yes, Mother."

By this time, the other clerks, who Nancy had sent to gather certain items she'd specified, had set them in the dressing room for Grace. They waved to their boss that the selections were hung for viewing. "We're ready for you now, Mrs. Knight."

"Please call me Vanessa." Grace patted Henrietta's shoulder. Smiling to calm the woman who sat muttering under her breath, fuming at the injustice recently observed, she followed Nancy.

When she entered her dressing area, she knew immediately that they had a problem. So far, she'd been making do with the huge closet full of expensive clothes that Vanessa had gathered. But this was different. It was to be Grace's day. Her wedding! And she meant to wear that which would suit her person and not just her body.

"I have no doubt that these choices would have suited me once, Nancy. But for this day, it needs to be a dress that will please my husband. I want a more traditional look—lace and pearls, full-skirted with a slight train and a sheer veil please. In other words, I want to look like a bride and not an entertainer." Waving her hand toward the sophisticated dresses chosen, Grace made her meaning as clear as possible.

Nancy, being a consummate actress—part of her shop training no doubt—hid her shock and answered quickly, "Of course Mrs...Vanessa. We received a new shipment of merchandise this morning, which I've just unpacked. There was one dress in particular, a lovely garment made with Brussels lace and studded with multiple gems. It will fit your shape perfectly."

Within a short time, Nancy helped Grace lift the lace wonder and it seemed as if it had been fashioned with her body in mind. Not seeing any price tag discomforted her somewhat. But, between Henrietta's gushing and the shop girls' sincere adulations, plus her own craving, she gave in and bought the dream dress for her special day.

***

Over the coming days, Tobias and Henrietta checked in with her repeatedly. Other than the strange moment of an inner struggle that day in the studio, Grace didn't have any other interaction with her nemesis to report.

Although she was relieved, at times the stress gnawed at her composure until she felt like she'd explode into a million pieces. And like the famous Humpty Dumpty, she'd never be put back together again.

Suspicions that her situation would soon blow up made her nervous as a patient in agony who'd run out of painkillers. No doubt, the fallout would be hellish and understanding this kept her on edge. Her even temper often became frayed and she found herself biting her tongue before overreacting.

With her nerves so on edge, an incident erupted that she normally wouldn't have instigated. After hearing another of Lucas's references to her bad behavior the day of the accident, she broke down and confronted him.

"Please tell me what happened on the day I crashed the car. Sometimes I have nightmares," she said. "But when I try to remember, there's blankness, nothing more."

"It's history, Vanessa. All's been forgiven, and I don't think we should talk about it and stir up possible problems." Firm in his resolution, Lucas gathered her into his arms and kissed away all her questions, leaving her filled with the frustration and also joy that his magical lips could create.

During those hectic days, Sammy began to act strangely. He refused to have his nanny read to him at night, or for that matter, anyone but Grace. He kicked up a fuss when his mother left the house for longer than a few hours. One day, it became so bad, that Lucas had to be called home from work to handle his naughtiness.

Finally caught up with her errands, and ready to start on the hospital ward when the day arrived, Grace had returned home, hoping to be able to spend some time with the boy. She walked into the house and found him in the den with his father. She heard Lucas's barely controlled anger which drew her to the doorway.

"Samuel, you will not refuse to listen to your nanny. This isn't the way you've been taught to behave. She's in charge of you, young man."

Grace's gaze fell on the youngster, whose bottom lip protruded in a way she'd never seen before. *What in the world?*

Sammy's arms were crossed over his chest and he wore a mutinous expression foreign to his happy nature. "Nanny's bossy."

"I pay her to be bossy. She's your teacher."

"She's old. I want to be with Mummy."

"Samuel Knight!" The roar made Grace wince, and she wondered how the boy could stand up to such authority. "What has gotten into you? You know you love your nanny."

This proved to be too much for the small youngster. He broke down and threw himself onto the cushions of the sofa. His little-boy hands covered his eyes and the howls of unhappiness made his small body shake with the emotions let loose. "I want my mummy!"

Grace's heart sped up and before she knew what had happened, she flew to Sammy and lifted him in her arms. "Lucas, he's very upset. Please stop yelling at him."

With his eyebrows meeting over stormy eyes, Lucas looked as if he would intervene with her cradling of the boy and instead pursed his lips and motioned for her to take a seat.

She sat and positioned the small boy on her knee. "Sammy-son, please stop crying. Mummy is here now." Her intentions were to put the boy away from her so she could see his face, but suddenly, it became impossible.

"Hold him! He needs us."

Another engulfed her, controlling her movements. Seemingly of their own accord, her hands caressed the boy, holding him so tightly that he began to struggle and still she couldn't force them to break their hold.

"Mummy, you're hurting me."

Lucas headed toward them, his face like a thundercloud.

Before she could stop it from happening, she pushed Sam away so fast, the little guy ended up on the floor. Vanessa, who had taken over for those few seconds, faded, but not before Grace heard an anguished, *"Oh God!"*

Quickly, before Lucas could, Grace reached out with a gentleness that drew the boy back to lean on her knees. He laid his head on her lap. This time she caressed his hair softly and said, "I'm sorry, Sammy, I was too rough. Tell me what has you so upset."

"I want *you,* Mummy."

"You want me? But I'm here."

"No! You go out all the time. I watch you from my room and you're always leaving me—like you used to."

"Oh, Sammy!" From deep inside, a scream reverberated that tore at the gentleness wrapping up Grace's soul. Never before had she heard such pain, and it certainly never existed inside her own head. Agony swelled and overwhelmed every nerve in her body until she yearned to have relief. If she could crawl away and hide—die even, she would. Only a little boy needed her, and for Grace, that took priority.

Lucas, sensing something wrong, slipped near her and tried to draw Sammy to him, but the boy refused to leave his mother.

"Are you angry with me again, Mummy? Have I been a bad boy?" His round green eyes, full of longing and tears, wouldn't hold hers and this alone broke her heart.

"Oh, Sammy. Why would you think that? Of course, I'm not angry with you." Shaking uncontrollably, her hand reached to wipe his cheeks.

"You never stay home and have tea with me and Nanny now. She says you're busy. But I think you don't like me anymore." The hiccups, interrupting his words, made the speech difficult to understand. His eyes awash with a continuous overflow finally looked at her and the fear she saw broke her heart. If the anguish burning inside her was any indication as to how his pain affected Vanessa, then Grace knew without a doubt that whatever her spirit-mate had done, she loved her child desperately.

"Can Mummy hug you again if I promise not to hold you too tight?"

In a flash, he climbed on her knee and she gathered him to her so he was cuddled close. She looked down into his face and purposely made sure he could see her expression. "Samuel Knight, you must listen to me carefully. I love you with all my heart. When I had my accident, there was damage to my head and it made me forget everything that happened to me before the time I woke up in the hospital. Remember, I explained this to you before?"

She waited for his reaction and accepted his nod that he had listened.

"Therefore, I can't explain to you why I sometimes behaved the way I did. My son, I don't think I was very nice, and for that I'm so dreadfully sorry. But it's different now, I'm different now. Do you understand? Do you have any questions?"

Sam shook his head, his eyes wide and listening.

Grace decided to take it one step further. She glanced at Lucas, who also seemed to be fascinated by her words. "After I woke up, I still didn't remember you, not until you came to see me. Then I realized that you were my miracle boy. I knew I loved you more than I ever thought possible and that I would do anything to make you happy. Do you believe me?"

With amazing intuitiveness, Sammy continued to stare into her eyes and then slowly, his head moved up and down. "Yes, Mummy."

"Therefore, I will explain to you why I've been so busy lately. Please pay attention, because I need you to understand, and then I will ask you for your blessing." Grace again looked toward Lucas and messaged him that he was included.

"While I was recuperating in the hospital, I saw how sympathetic the nurses were to me and others who were sick and scared. People, who had to be away from their families, who needed someone to take care of them. We all required help from these hard-working women. My own nurses treated me with such kindness, that I decided I wanted to be just like them and look after others myself one day. I knew if I studied for a degree at the hospital where they teach people like me, then one day I, too, could be a nurse. Sammy, all the time I've been away from home, I was organizing this training." She put her hands on both sides of his face and watched his reaction. "I know doing this will make *me* happy. But... and listen closely, nothing is more important than *your* happiness. If my being away so much is going to upset you, I will wait to take this schooling until you feel more comfortable with the idea."

Sammy wiped at his wet eyes with the back of his hand and then used his shirt front to get rid of the damp. His small shoulders straightened as he sat upright. The intelligence in his gaze had her bursting with pride. "Can I come to see your school one day?"

After he heard the soft sob she couldn't hold back, Lucas answered. "Sure you can, Sam. In fact, we both must visit Mummy at the hospital so we can see where she'll be working. I'm very proud of her, and I think her menfolk need to support her. She'll be working very hard on her lessons and the classes will take up a fair amount of her time and energy."

Sam turned back to her. "Will you have time to read me stories before I go to bed?" His earnest questioning earned him a kiss on his cheeks both from Grace and his dad.

Grace grinned. "Absolutely! I enjoy your bedtime stories. It's our special time together. And, Sammy-son, I'll be here as often as I can. Also, you have my promise to let you know each day what I have on my schedule so you'll always know where I am. Okay?"

"Okay, Mummy." Sammy kissed her cheek and sat back with a smile. "Can I have my tea now?"

Breathing a huge sigh of relief, Grace tickled him and laughed at his giggles. "Tea it shall be, my lad." She held out her hand to Lucas. "Come, Daddy, we have a very hungry boy."

As the three walked to the kitchen together, a satisfied hum from inside let her know another had been soothed as well. Only now, Grace knew damn well, it was time to meet the enemy face to face. So to speak!!

Chapter 30

As soon as she could sneak away that evening, Grace went to the one place where she knew Vanessa would have a hard time staying away. The smell of the paint thinner attacked her from the minute she stepped into the studio and sat down on the stool in front of the painting.

"We need to talk, Vanessa. You must see that now." Grace knew she didn't have to speak out loud. Dr. Andrews had explained that they would be able to converse through their thoughts. Although a headache loomed, she still strained to travel inwards.

Unfortunately, access to the other occupant stayed firmly closed. Grace decided to prompt her. She picked up the tool she'd been forced to use the last time she'd sat in front of this portrait and began to brush away at the edges with no skill whatsoever.

Instantaneously, Vanessa seeped in. "For heaven's sake, stop that. You'll ruin a precious work of art with your clumsiness."

Aha! *"Then as the expert, you must teach me how it's done."*

"Look, whoever you are, the only thing I want to teach you is how to kill us and get it over with."

"Like you tried on the night of the crash?"

"What's it to you? Other than fact that you've stolen what doesn't belong to you and taken over my body as if I had no rights. Without your interference, I'd be exactly where I should be now— in my grave."

"You see! That's what I don't understand. You could have recovered. I know it and so do you. But you chose to die."

"That's my right."

"I didn't say it wasn't."

"Then why did you interfere?"

"Because, I did die! Look, my name is Grace Joye. I'm a nurse who had a brain tumor. I passed on while we were still in the hospital. I mean my body—"

"I know what you mean. What I want to know is who gave you the right to take over mine?"

"At the time, I believed your brain had expired, and, as crazy as this sounds, that you had no need for your perfectly good body."

"And you did."

"Yes." Grace kneaded her fingers and knew her anxiety was obvious to Vanessa. "I never realized you might still be alive inside there, or I wouldn't have let this happen."

"Yes, you would, or at least your sidekicks would have made it happen. That Dr. Andrews is a wily old fart, isn't he? And there's just no words to explain away Mrs. Dorn."

"He's not an old fart. And she's lovely."

"See, I knew there was a good reason for us not to cohabit. And after what happened earlier today, I'm positive we need to end this connection."

"Do you mean when you hugged your son?"

A well of pain flooded inside and Grace's stomach walls stiffened with resentment. The voice inside increased alarmingly. "I was referring to when I threw my son to the floor.

That's what I meant, you stupid bitch. I hurt him—again." A sob escaped before Vanessa began to fade.

"Please don't go. Sammy was fine. I stopped you before any real damage occurred. Vanessa, listen. I'd never let anything happen to the boy. Never!" Grace waited for an answer and only emptiness emerged. *"Don't ignore me, Vanessa. Please. We need to discuss our future."*

Suddenly, heaviness filled her, and Grace knew Vanessa was back. Despite the few seconds of relief when she returned, her words left a horrible residue of fear.

"Can't you get it through your head? We have no future."

Chapter 31

With the words *"We have no future"* ringing in her head, the next few days were hellish for Grace. Her whole life had been about helping others. Being kind and understanding to those in need of comfort. And now, deep in the very core of her existence, she experienced such utter desolation, it was all she could do to make herself get out of bed in the morning.

Lucas tried very hard to cheer her with flowers and loving kindness, but it didn't help at all. In fact, the harder he tried, the more her rival forced her detachment and she pushed him away. Earlier that day, he'd come across her sitting alone and staring out the window at the heavy clouds blocking the sunshine, turning her bedroom into a dark cave. She hadn't allowed the housekeeper, Mrs. Platt, entrance to light the fire, and damp oozed through the room leaving a musty odor.

Lucas turned on the bedside lamp and fussed at the fireplace until a cheery flame began to dispel the cold. Grace fought with Vanessa and stopped her from yelling at him to get out.

"Vanessa, let me take you for a ride, away from the house. It's been days since you shut yourself in here. It's not like you, my love."

Before Grace could answer, Vanessa stepped up. "What do you know about me and what I like? You hate me."

Eyes narrowed, Lucas hesitated before reaching out. "Please don't do this again, Vanessa." He tried a smile and, in a teasing way, he said, "Don't revert to the old you. I like the new Vanessa so much better."

Grace recognized the anger exploding and before she could gather her wits to stop Vanessa from striking, she spit out words that could never be reclaimed. "The new Vanessa is an imposter..." Grace stopped the next utterances from being unleashed and spoke herself. "Give me time, Lucas. I need to be alone for a while longer."

Obvious concern fought with his respect for her choices, and respect won. "I'm here for you, darling. I will do whatever you need. Just please, don't leave us again." He kissed her mouth with a gentleness that almost ripped her apart for wanting to be in his arms. The strength of Vanessa's influence stopped that from happening.

Each day, they descended lower into a morass of depression. Despite her struggles to stop herself from sinking, she couldn't fight the power that Vanessa wove through her will. When it came right down to it, she just didn't have the strength needed to take over from the powerful spirit fighting for control.

She forgot about the approaching wedding. And ignored the assignments that were necessary for her to start her schooling, though the time drew closer. Whenever she thought about it, her mind wavered and sunk back into morose emptiness.

The only time she did gather enough courage to fight

her way free was each night, when she fulfilled her promise to read Sam his bedtime stories. During these wonderfully cozy moments, Vanessa lurked but let Grace take over.

Every time she held the small boy in her arms, kissed his cheek, caressed his hair and smelled his wonderful just-bathed freshness, Grace felt Vanessa creep out and experience those moments with her. Warmth exuded, and a low hum of delight eased over their combined spirits. But she wouldn't stick around for long, and these maneuvers started a sickness growing inside that Grace hated and Vanessa reveled in.

Even though Grace recognized that they were heading for a fall, it was as if she was powerless to stop it from happening. All she could do was pray that she might prevent the inevitable.

A few days later, after dinner, Vanessa began to dress in outdoor clothes. She gathered up the necessary items to go out of the house.

"*Where are we going?*" Grace had no idea.

"*I need a drink. And to get out of here before I go mad.*"

"*We have a bar in the sitting room. Lucas would be happy to have drinks with us.*"

"*Can't you get it through your thick skull? I hate that man. He wrecked my life. If he hadn't gotten me pregnant, we might still be happy. Now, I'll never forgive the bastard.*"

While talking, they made their way to the car and Grace felt terror begin to build in the darkness. "*You love Sammy. And don't pretend otherwise, because I know better.*"

They drove through the night, with Vanessa steering. "*Yes, of course I love Sam. He's the only one I care about in this whole rotten world. But I'm bad for him. Don't you see? I'll hurt him. I have before, and I'll do it again. I'm evil!*"

A sob broke through, and for what seemed like an eternity, Vanessa let down her guard. Memories exploded inside, horrific images that made Grace think she'd be sick. "*My God!*"

Shivers of apprehension took hold that made Grace pay attention to where they were and how the trees flew past the window. Their car raced down the country lane at a dangerous speed. Was this where Vanessa crashed her car the last time? She seemed to remember Lucas and the doctors talking about this area and, all of a sudden, she just knew.

Vanessa gripped the wheel and pressed down hard on the gas pedal.

Grace realized she only had seconds to make a difference. With every ounce of determination, she compelled their foot to ease. They fought each other while the car swerved from one side of the road to the other. Thankfully, no other vehicles approached as the battle continued. Grace shouted, "*Oh, no you don't, my girl! No silliness. No more crashes, Vanessa. I mean it!*"

"*You have no right to stop me. I have to end it, stop this pain. I can't bear it any longer.*"

"*You're not alone anymore, Vanessa. I'm here with you. Please don't hurt us. Don't make Lucas and Sam suffer any more.*"

"*You're an imposter. I hate you. I hate my life. Let me go!*"

"*No! Vanessa, please listen. If you kill us, Sammy will grow up thinking his mummy hated him. Sometimes, he believes it to be true now. With suicide to deal with, he'll never be normal. You know our little boy. He'll believe we didn't care, that we don't love him. How could you leave him with that legacy?*"

Chapter 32

"Oh, God!" Vanessa keened. *"I never thought about it like that. You're right."*

Vanessa sunk into total despair. She just let go. Grace lifted their foot off the gas and pulled over to the edge of the road. Her body shook so badly she could only hold on to the wheel and wait. Breathing hard, pulse ramped dangerously high, it was hard to stay conscious; she slouched and let their body relax. Once the panic receded, Grace began to gently delve into the horrific images Vanessa had shared. *"Your mother was a wicked, wicked woman, Vanessa. You poor baby, how did you stand the brutality?"*

"The worst part was that she loved to torment me. The beatings and burnings were nothing beside the mental abuse. Her evilness knew no bounds. Nothing restricted her sense of decency."

"You must talk to a professional, you know that."

"Who would listen to me raving about a childhood that was so steeped in the darkness, that just thinking about some of what went on is enough to send me over the edge."

"*My dear, you make my heart weep. Such cruelty! In all my days as a nurse, not once did I see such wickedness as what you survived. Never! And I've been overcome many times with the immorality of human behavior while working in Casualty.*"

"*With your words about Samuel... Sammy, you've effectively destroyed any chance I have for peace. How can I leave him thinking he wasn't loved? Especially after seeing how beautifully he responded to you. Can't you see what you've done?*"

"*Vanessa, I know you don't have a lot of respect for Dr. Andrews—*"

"*You mean the wily old fart?*"

Lightness entered their discussion for a brief second and Grace responded instantly. She giggled uncontrollably before gaining restraint. "*Yes! He is that. But he's also the most intelligent, gentle and kindhearted man in the universe. He will listen, Vanessa. And he will help us find peace for you. Then you can live your life to the fullest. Once you're secure, I'll fade into the space you've been occupying. It's I who have no right to your body.*"

"*No! Don't you dare! Listen, it's your fault that I'm still alive at all. Maybe one day I can be alone with Sammy, when he's older, but I don't trust the blackness not to come back. I'll revert to 'her'. You've seen it happen. I have no control.*"

"*But I do. Between the two of us, we can survive anything.*"

Vanessa started the car. She pulled from the side of the road, turned back the way they'd come and drove at a moderate speed.

Grace overflowed with relief. "*Oh, good. We're going home.*"

"*Not yet. I want some wine. And I need to think.*"

Feeling the lighter side of Vanessa, Grace relaxed. "*You know what? I could use one myself. I wonder if we should order two?*" The thought made her chuckle and she recognized that hysteria lurked very close.

Vanessa sighed, and Grace knew she smiled. *"You'll drink whatever I order, and like it."*

Chapter 33

As they approached the drinking establishment; through the window Grace saw a whiskered old codger wiping away imaginary spills on the spotless bar. *Freddie!* He'd visited her on the ward during her recuperation. Now, she understood where he'd met Vanessa. Which made Grace feel rather sad. That the only person who'd come to visit Vanessa in hospital, beside her family, was the bartender who'd served her drinks.

His head lifted as the bell over the door rang. At first, shock registered. But then his eyes lit up and he made a fuss over them in the charmingly playful way that older men can pass off as attractive and fun.

"Vanessa! Me hearts lifted for seeing yer pretty face, so 'tis."

"Get way with you, Fred. You say that to all the girls."

"But I don't mean it with the others. Not like with you, me love."

Vanessa made a face, and Grace rejoiced in the slightly upbeat feeling emanating from the other woman. "Can you bring me a glass of my favorite wine and quit working so hard on getting a tip?"

"Yer a hard-hearted woman, my darlin'. Be right there."

Hovering in the background, Grace let Vanessa lead their movements and paid strict attention to her demeanor. Other than a sincere smile to Freddie, she paid no attention at all to the many appreciative glances she drew from males at various tables.

One woman, returning to her chair from the loo, tried a smile as she passed and was met with a stony glare.

"That wasn't very nice."

"What wasn't nice?" Vanessa slid into a booth, arranged her handbag on the seat and retrieved a few quid from her wallet.

"The way you treated that woman. She smiled at you and you glared back. She meant no harm."

"I don't like women."

Grace understood instantly why Vanessa would make such a statement and so she backed off. *"Is that why you chose your job? I mean, I know you have incredible talent, but you work alone, away from others."*

"I guess so. I've never been able to stand being in close proximity with other females. Especially if they wear certain perfumes."

Remembering the images from Vanessa's memories, Grace knew Vanessa's mother had dressed like a whore and smelled like she'd bathed in musk. Grace could sympathize.

Freddie approached with her glass of wine and leaned over to whisper. "I sure could have used yer help behind the bar earlier. Things are much quieter now."

"Call if you need me. I've escaped for a few hours, so not to worry."

Freddie winked and reached to pat her arm very lightly.

He hesitated to make sure his touch would be welcome.

Then the door's bell rang again and Grace saw Henrietta bustle into the room as if in a hurry.

Vanessa let out a cuss and tried to fade but Grace urged her not to. *"Please stay."*

"I can't stand the woman! She's ugly. With that unsightly wart on the end of her nose and her frizzy hair, truth to tell, she gives me the willies."

"Look into her eyes. She's everything that's good in the world."

Once Henrietta spotted Grace, she beetled her way over and enveloped Grace in her loving arms.

Vanessa cringed inside but she didn't go away. Instead she lurked in the background and watched.

"I've been that worried about you, pet. Lucas called in a panic, saying you were gone and he had no idea where. I remembered Vanessa used to come here sometimes and so I took the chance. Himself's coming as soon as he gets free from his hospital rounds."

"Why were you so worried, Henrietta?"

The housekeeper stared at Grace and her eyes filled. Ernest, full of sincere adoration, the love she presented would have healed anyone's pain to some extent. "Don't be daft, dearie. You know you've not bin yerself lately. I don't wish to intrude, but we've all been sick at heart, scared that you-know-who might have come back and taken over." During the last of her sentence, Mrs. Dorn moved in closer and whispered.

Vanessa snorted and Grace had to laugh. "Henrietta, you-know-who is always with me. And you mustn't judge her by her actions. Look, we've all been less than understanding about her part in this situation. After all, it's I who invaded her body and used it for my own."

"Well, the silly chit didn't want it, did she?" Like a

mother cat, Henrietta spit her defiance. At the same time as she reached for Grace's hand. "She's there now, ain't she?"

"Yes. She's listening to us talk."

"Well, put her on, 'cause I'd like a few words with her."

Vanessa openly laughed, as did Grace. "I'm not a telephone, Henrietta. You can just say what you want."

"Cor... but you'll be listening."

"I don't have to, if you'd rather I didn't."

Mrs. Dorn bit her lip and thought for a few seconds. Then she replied. "No matter. I just wanted to plead with the girl not to hurt you. From what I understand by talking with my ol' pal Freddie, the woman doesn't like females. What she doesn't know is that yer the best mate anyone could ask fer and she'd better take care with you, or she'll answer to me, so she will."

Before Grace could speak and tell her old friend just how touched she was, Vanessa kicked in and took over. "So, what is it you think you could do to me, old woman?"

Eyes narrowing, chin quivering in indignation, Henrietta snarled, "Jist don't you try me, missie. You have one friend in the world: Freddie. And he happens to be an old beau of mine. Whose side do you think he would choose if we started a war?"

Astounded, Grace had never seen this side of Henrietta before. The meanness in her hard tone, her unshakeable manner, it was like that of a cynical copper making an arrest. Her quivering cheeks certainly didn't belie the threat in her eyes.

Vanessa turned inward. "So... I did as you asked. I looked into her eyes."

"Don't take her wrong. She's not normally like this. I don't know what's gotten into her."

"She's protecting you. And I think it's one of the most beautiful things I've ever witnessed. She takes my breath away. And, you're right. Her eyes are wonderful."

Relieved that Vanessa understood, Grace relaxed. *"She's the best friend in the world. I'm—we're very lucky."*

Vanessa answered Henrietta. This time, her voice had taken on a rare timbre that Grace had only heard her use when talking to or about Sammy.

"Mrs. Dorn. I won't take your friend away from you. In fact, I've begged her to stay for good. I hate this world and everything about it, except for my son. So you won't be seeing a lot of me in the future."

"Bollocks! Don't be daft."

Vanessa laughed out loud. And then she listened.

"Bless my soul, there's no proper reason you shouldn't live along with Grace. My girl's got enough heart for the two of you. If you ask me, life's too precious to give it away for good."

"I appreciate that you're trying to help, Mrs. Dorn. And you are right. There were certain areas in my life that pleased me: my work and my son. But nothing else held any appeal and I'd just as soon let Grace look after those areas."

"Good! Yer smart and I might be able to like you. We must visit again. Now, can you put Grace back on?"

"She wants to speak with you." Vanessa's spirit had lightened considerable.

"I'm not coming back, Vanessa. Mrs. Dorn is right. You need to live your own life. Goodness me, I've just realized what I've done to you. How terribly I've acted! I've taken over your life as if I had every right. From now on, you must deal with everything, and with the help of Dr. Andrews and Mrs. Dorn, you'll do just fine. Please find it in your heart to be kind to Lucas. Try and

learn to love him again. And, whatever you do, keep our Sammy happy. Good-bye."

Chapter 34

"I can't. She's gone!"

Never before had Vanessa felt so alone and frightened. Even as a child, when she'd had to face down a vicious woman who liked to inflict pain, her brain hadn't screamed this uncontrollably to stop the torture.

Henrietta spoke soothingly. "There, there, pet. What do you mean, she's gone?"

"For some reason, she's decided she stole my life. Now, just like that, she's giving it back to me. I'm serious, Mrs. Dorn, whatever will I do?"

Mrs. Dorn reached for Vanessa's hands and patted them. "Bleedin' hell! Me and my big mouth. She's taken my words to heart and decided she's cheated you, hasn't she?"

"How did you know?"

Mrs. Dorn lifted her heavy knitted, hot-pink handbag onto the table and shuffled through the contents. With a "blimey, ere tis", she whipped out a small photograph album and opened it to the page where a young woman lay comatose on a hospital bed. The left side of her face,

disfigured by a huge bluish-red birthmark, showed clearly
in the photograph. As did her slight body and fine brown
curls.

There were other shots of Grace, but this first one
emphasized the dreadful blemish she lived with all her
life. The last image was when she'd worked on a case with
Doctor Andrews. Sitting in their kitchen, sharing a cup
of tea with Henrietta, she was laughing. The light behind
graced her with a glow and presented her loveliness in a
way that drew one's attention to her gentle smile.

"This is our Gracie. She suffered all her life because of
her face. As you can see, she was a sensitive, gentle soul,
and wouldn't take anything she felt didn't belong to her.
Me 'n my big mouth just reminded her that she did just
that."

"Well, she didn't take anything I wanted to keep. You
must help me get her back." Terror began to slide inside of
Vanessa, and she knew it was just a matter of time before
she'd revert to being the bitch she always hated.

Before either of them could say more, Dr. Andrews
arrived.

"Oh, Doctor, I'm most terribly sorry, but I've flubbed
it good this time." With very few words, a lot of hand
wringing and some tears, Henrietta explained what had
just happened. Dr. Andrews listened without saying a
word. Then he patted his housekeeper's shoulder, passed
her his hankie and said, "I'd love a cup of coffee, my dear.
And don't you worry. We'll straighten out Grace in no
time at all."

While Henrietta went to Freddie for his coffee, Dr.
Roberts took the bench abandoned by Mrs. Dorn and
smiled at Vanessa. "Hello, Mrs. Knight."

Remembering Grace's words, Vanessa swallowed away

her normal reaction to a stranger and instead she spoke. "Please, you must help me. You're her friend. Talk to Grace. Make her come back."

Charming as always, Dr. Andrews spoke soothingly, while smiling with warmth and understanding.

"But she's there, right inside you."

"No! She's shut down completely. I can't reach her. It's like there's a huge void of emptiness where she once existed." Vanessa heard her voice rise and knew hysteria was close to taking over.

Again, Dr. Andrews spoke calmly and used the words that he must have known would ease her fear. "Vanessa, I hope you don't mind me being personal, but I feel as if we already know each other. So, my dear, the woman who has become so important to you is still there. Just like you were when she first inhabited your body. And we both know, if you were in turmoil or danger, she wouldn't be able to help herself in saving you. But, we also know that she feels she's stealing your life. Have I got that part correct?"

Vanessa heard his words and knew he did understand. "Yes. But I don't want it."

"Are you sure? Have you lived without the pain I clearly see in your eyes? Dealt with your past that must have been horrid to put those shadows there?"

"Trust me, Doctor. I'm flawed. Terribly flawed. The only peace I've known was while I rested in a coma in the hospital. I loved those quiet moments and I yearn to be back there. I don't want the frustration, the utter agony of having to deal with my life."

"You've almost got me persuaded. But I'm afraid it's Grace who you must convince. Until she knows that you've done everything to get on with trying to live normally, she won't be swayed. With that part, I can help you."

Relapsing to her earlier behavior, Vanessa spat her wrath. "Help me? God, don't you get it, old man? Nothing and no one can help me. I'm a lost cause."

"You think so? Well, Grace needs you now. And so does your husband and your son. You can act out like before, or you can come to my office tomorrow, be prepared to work hard and we'll start analyzing your past and the reasons behind your conduct. I can't promise an overnight cure, Vanessa, but with treatment, we can give you some peace. I truly believe that Grace knew this must be done and is forcing your hand."

Vanessa, who'd sat back down, bowed her head into her hands and sighed. "She's never going to believe me until I've dealt with these nightmares, is she?"

"No. I truly don't believe so. She's a smart lady. If she feels that you can heal with my help, then we must follow her lead."

Chapter 35

Over the next few weeks, Vanessa tried understanding the medical jargon that Dr. Andrews used to explain her psychotic behavior. None of it mattered or made sense to her. All she knew was how desperate she was for Grace to rescue her. Aware of a strange inner peace, absent before the accident, Vanessa knew Grace was helping in her own way. But it just wasn't good enough.

Pure exhaustion attacked her after each session. Almost physically ill, she came close to total collapse. To make the treatments easier, Dr. Andrews resorted to hypnotherapy and that seemed to help. Other times, he listened while she ranted and screamed her fury, describing the utter torture she'd suffered as a mere child.

Since she'd never visited these memories—in fact, quite the opposite—reliving the instances left her drained, miserable and totally unequipped to handle the pressure she was living under.

Without the frequent hugs from Mrs. Dorn and the constant encouragement from Dr. Andrews, and the sleeping medications he prescribed, she had no doubt she'd have attempted another car accident.

By being absent most of the time, at home she managed to hide a lot of her struggles. Each night, her indulgence was reading to Sam. At first, fear stopped her from sitting too close to him, using a cold as her reason. But eventually, she came to kneel by the side of his bed, lean over and read him his favorite Beatrix Potter stories. These were the times that kept her from giving up altogether; knowing how delighted her son was with having a mummy who loved him. As dead inside as she often felt, he was her one light in that horrific darkness.

With Dr. Andrews' help, they explained to Lucas that she'd had a small relapse and would need further therapy. Despite Vanessa's belief that he'd sensed her return, she continued to play Grace's role. Many times she'd watch his eyes narrow when she'd refuse to look at him or see his hands clench when she reverted unthinkingly to her earlier behavior.

She refused all physical interaction and knew she hurt his feelings from her rejections. That couldn't be helped. Letting him put his hands on her now would drive her over the edge. When life got too hard, she would slink into her studio, lock the door and lose herself in her work. The portrait was close to being finished, and a small feeling of pride grew for what she'd been able to accomplish.

Lucas caught up with her one evening as she was on the verge of retiring. "Vanessa, you haven't been answering your mail and the hospital finally got in touch with me today. They've held your place on the nursing program as long as possible, but without any further communication from you personally, they will have to refill the opening."

"What did you tell them?"

"That you've been unwell and won't be up to taking any

nursing training at this time. What else could I say? I know how much it meant to you, so I did ask for them to transfer your application to the next available opening."

"Yes, that's fine. You said the right thing. I couldn't take on any classes right now. I... I'm sorry Lucas. It's been a hellish few weeks. Bear with me for a while longer. I'm trying so hard."

"Yes. I can see how traumatic life has become for you recently. Are you sure you should continue the sessions with Dr. Andrews? Seems to me that ever since you've begun seeing the man professionally, you've become even more unhappy."

"Oh, Lucas, he's actually the only thing keeping me sane. I can't explain it to you, but I do so need his help and yours."

Softening, the harsh lines on his face fading, Lucas reached for her. His hand dropped when she flinched, but his tone stayed gentle. "My darling wife, I want to be there for you in any way that I can. I've followed Dr. Andrews's advice and given you the space you seem to desperately crave. And if you need me for anything else, by God, I will try my damnedest to come through for you. Please... just ask and it's yours. I can't lose you again, Vanessa. Not after what we've come to mean to each other. Don't do that to me, or Sammy."

Vanessa felt a jolt inside and knew his voice had reached Grace where others had failed dismally. She tucked this information away to share with her two conspirators and gently bade Lucas goodnight.

"One more thing, Vanessa. Your wedding dress arrived today, and I had Mrs. Platt hang it in your room."

Chapter 36

Lucas walked away from his wife and noted the instant shock she couldn't hide when she heard his message about her wedding dress.

Confound it! He hoped she intended to go through with their wedding plans. He'd never seen his little boy so excited about anything. Wearing a tux like his dad gave Sammy bragging rights to anyone who would listen.

The staff, both at work and here at home, were quietly going about their duties, putting this party together so it could happen in the bountiful gardens surrounding the house. The big day was this coming Saturday and the weather promised to be lovely—the kind of day any bride willed to happen for such a special occasion. He remembered when they'd first discussed the event, Vanessa's excitement to be remarried had lifted him so high, and it was those memories that kept him planning.

He'd organized the caterers, the church, and flowers, even a band, leaving Vanessa worry-free. Everyone had been invited weeks before, and all was in readiness. Everything, but the bride.

Truthfully, Lucas wasn't sure whether Vanessa was even aware of the building pressure the rest of the house felt with the day approaching so quickly. Despite what the woman had been going through, he knew it would break his heart if she reneged on renewing their vows. Only by facing her in front of Vicar Witherby and announcing their love for each other could he continue with this farce. Her vows would be the convincing factor; words that she'd speak for him alone.

With both hands holding the back of his neck, head down and leaning against the wall, Lucas felt another headache building. He wondered if he should remind Dr. Andrews about the approaching event. Invitations had been sent out, but that had been some time ago.

He knew the physiatrist worked continuously each day with Vanessa, helping her with drug treatments and therapy. When Lucas had demanded explanations, Dr. Andrews had briefly explained that her case history was extensive and difficult, leading back to shocking problems as a child. Other than that small bit of information, he kept their sessions private. Lucas respected his assessment and his knowledge. The man could be relied on. He knew so because he was the only one Vanessa trusted. And therefore, he had to trust him also.

Through this hellish period of time, all Lucas really wanted was his gentle Vanessa back. The same woman who had woken up in the hospital. The girl who had loved him so beautifully that he'd walked on air for weeks. How could he and Sam live without her? It was like having a taste of the most delicious steak, and then learning your diet for the rest of your life would be potatoes.

Good God, please don't do this to me!

The wraith who lived in his house today, reminded him

so much of the old Vanessa. Every so often, he got a glimpse of her previous anger and vicious nature. Then, just as quickly, it would fade and her lifeless face would reappear, with nothing lighting it but sadness.

There was only one thing that kept him going through this nightmare. Every so often when her guard was down, he'd see a flash of the woman he loved, blazing from her eyes—an intensity of feeling emanating from her spirit.

He only prayed that when she faced him in front of God and all their friends to renew her vows, her gentle nature would light up and he'd have her back—the woman he now loved with all his heart. The one he secretly thought of as Grace—his sweet angel.

Chapter 37

"You don't mean it?" Vanessa screamed at the G.P. who'd just given her the horrible news. "I can't be pregnant. I hate being pregnant."

False sympathy shielded the disgust that flashed instantaneously when she reacted. "I'm sorry you feel that way, Mrs. Knight. Dr. Andrews wanted me to give you an examination before he was willing to put you on stronger medications and it's a good thing he did so. You mustn't take any of the heavy prescriptions he intended to try. They would be harmful to the child."

"Then you have to get rid of it."

Coldly, the doctor replied. "I'm afraid that's impossible. Other than your frail mental state, you are very healthy. There are laws against ending a viable pregnancy, as you very well know."

Losing patience with the idiot who wasn't listening, Vanessa shouted. "I don't care. I can't do this again. I suffered horribly after the birth of my first child. No one can expect me to have another."

"I'm not sure what you mean. Was the birth that

difficult? There is pain relief that we can administer during the procedure."

"No, you don't understand." Weeping into her handkerchief, she raised her eyes to see his reaction. "I feared for my son's life."

"Goodness gracious. Why?"

"Because he was in jeopardy."

"In jeopardy? Good God! From whom?"

"Me!"

Chapter 38

"I can't go through with this. Mrs. Dorn. You must go and put a stop to this madness." Leaning against the window in her bedroom, Vanessa shoved aside the curtains and looked out over the lawn where the florists were setting up the final touches to the beautifully decorated gardens. The setting for the party shone with glorious flower arrangements, satin ribbons and white chiffon.

Sweeping her hand from the view outside, to the bed—where a dazzling vision of white lace lay draped over the quilt—she made sure the housekeeper knew what she meant.

Mrs. Dorn's mouth dropped open and she wiped her hands across the front of her silk, ruffled, cherry-colored dress as if she were wiping flour off while baking. "Vanessa, pet, I thought we agreed that you were going to do this. I don't wish to upset you, dearie, but you discussed it with himself. Remember?"

"You need to go and get Dr. Andrews. I want him right now. This is insane. It must stop. It all must stop. I don't want to have a baby! I don't want to marry Lucas. I just want to be left alone..."

"Now that'd be a bit of a sticky wicket, it would. Bleeding hell, what will everyone say? You'll more 'n likely break Lucas's heart. Think of Sammy. I've never seen the lad so keen."

"I don't care. I can't—I just can't!"

Before Mrs. Dorn could answer, the door flew open and the little guy himself appeared and ran straight up to her. "Mummy, I came to give you my wedding present."

Instinct took over before she put on the brakes. An urge to hit out overwhelmed her instantaneously. Thank God, something held her hand after it lifted. Was it Grace? Or, had she controlled herself? She bit her lip and slid onto a chair to recover from knees unwilling to hold her upright.

From the corner of her eye, she'd seen Mrs. Dorn reach out for the boy but still her hand when Vanessa calmed her reaction. Clutching her fingers together for safety, Vanessa held back the threatening tears, the screams of frustration and the horror at being so vile. Instead, she forced a smile to welcome him closer.

An envelope noticeable in the hand he held out caught her attention. "Is this for me?"

"Ye-yes. Are you okay?" He hesitated and watched her closely.

"I'm fine, Sam. Let me see what you've got there." She smiled from her heart.

He moved closer and then leaned against her knee. "I made it for you. Daddy helped me with the writing, but I drew the picture by myself."

Once opened, the drawing revealed a portrait of her done by the hands of a very talented child. He'd gotten the shape of her face correct; the hair was mostly curls the way that children loved to color but her eyes were what mesmerized. Even at his age, he'd managed to show the sadness lurking in her smile. The raw talent delighted her, and she knew instantly that he had the gift that she didn't. If mentored properly, he could be a terrific artist.

She reached out to take his small hands in hers. 'One day, Samuel, you will be a fine painter. You must study hard. I'm very proud of your talent, and I will always cherish this beautiful picture. Thank you, darling."

Precious small arms wound around her neck and almost brought her to her knees. But she fought off the stressful sickness and smiled as he ran to the door. "We're going to get married today. You, me and Daddy! It'll be super. You must get ready. I'm going now to put on my tuxedo, the same as Daddy's. I'll see you soon." With that, he slammed the door and was gone.

Grace!

Moments passed and nothing.

Mrs. Dorn took one look at her face and fled also. "I'll get you the doctor."

Grace!!

Chapter 39

Silence...

Vanessa broke down completely. *"Grace, I beg you! You must see the truth now. I'm broken, damaged and not safe to be a mother. If you make me continue this farce, I'll most likely end up in an insane asylum, taking drugs to keep me alive."*

Silence...

"Please come out and talk with me. Can't you see? You're forcing me into a hellish existence. I can't stand it! I don't want it! My God, Grace. Not another baby?"

A lightness began to sift into her body and Vanessa stopped tearing at her hair and raking her hands across her face. *"Shh, be calm, Vanessa. Did you really say we're having another baby?"*

"Thank the Lord. You've come back."

"I never left. I just closed myself off so you could have your life back."

Leaning back in her chair, her body unwinding from the tenseness of just a few moments earlier, Vanessa spoke more honestly than she'd ever done before. *"If you don't understand anything else, Grace, you must understand this. I don't want my life back. I was never happier than when you were with me, taking care of me. I've tried, Grace, really I have. You must believe me. Dr. Andrews and Mrs. Dorn have helped me tremendously. But I couldn't go through having another baby. Terrified I'll hurt the child. Unable to stifle that disgusting anger that flares up before I even know it'll erupt because it springs out uncontrollably. This is truly yours and Lucus's baby. You are the rightful mother. Please, Grace, you must never leave again."*

"Vanessa, be calm my dear. Don't go on so. You're breaking my heart. I never meant for you to suffer when I left you to live your life. It made me so happy, I couldn't believe, given time and treatment, you wouldn't eventually be happy also. Being loved by Lucas, living day to day as Sammy's mother, it's your right not mine."

"Yes, well, I don't love Lucas. Most times I can barely stand to be in the same room as him. And he knows it and has been very unhappy since you left. The only reason he's going along with this farce wedding re-enactment is for Sam's sake. When we're together, he's cold and withdrawn. And there isn't anything I can do to change him. Only you can undo the damage I've created. And you must. You really must. I do so want them to be happy again."

Grace sensed Vanessa's panic rising and she released a huge torrent of tenderness throughout their spirit.

Tears beginning to dry, Vanessa sighed. *"Let me seek the peace I crave. I beg you."*

"Yes, but on one condition. Once this child is born—and I hope more will follow—Sam will need to feel special from time to time. Only one person can give that to him—a mother who understands his talent as an artist and his individual needs. As he grows older, he'll need you and you must promise to be there for him."

This time, a blissful glow stemmed from Vanessa. "Of

course! Nothing would make me happier. Thank you, Grace. Now you must put on your lovely dress and get ready for this special event. I'll rest now."

Happiness flooded Grace and she knew her friend was finally at peace.

The door burst open and Henrietta lumbered into the room followed by a concerned Dr. Andrews. "See there, Doctor. I told you. She just sits and stares out the window, like a zombie—all cold and unmoving."

"Calm down, Mrs. Dorn. I'll speak with her." Dr. Andrews knelt in front of Vanessa and gently took her hand. Suddenly, she linked her fingers with his and said, "Tobias, I'm so glad you're here."

Falling into a near-faint on the chair across from Grace's, legs sprawled and skirt dipping to the floor, Mrs. Dorn put her hands together and screeched. "Praise the Lord! She's back!"

Chapter 40

"Help me with my dress, Henrietta, will you, dear?"

"Blimey, Grace," Henrietta's tears flooded her face and didn't seem to have a shut-off valve, "it's so glad I am to have you back. I don't wish to speak ill of the departed, but Vanessa was a sorry soul, miserable in her unhappiness. And you're such a ray of sunshine. I've missed yer company, pet. That I have."

"Thank you, Henrietta. I think we must hurry along now. Tobias said the guests have all arrived at the church and Vicar Witherby is waiting for the bride."

"Yer dress is a little snug, luv. It's difficult to do up all the buttons. There, I've got 'em now. Let me place the veil on your hair."

They appeared together in the looking glass, the glowing younger woman with the chubby housekeeper behind. Both beamed with joy, sharing a moment Grace would never forget.

The knock at the door sent Henrietta flying. "If that's your intended, I'll send him on his way. He mustn't see you until you join him at the altar."

The door handle began to open before Henrietta could stop it and Sammy's head peeked in timidly. "Mummy, are you almost ready? Dr. Andrews said I was to come and get you. He said that you needed an escort?"

Henrietta beamed at the child as she rushed past. "You'll be the perfect lad to escort your mother, Master Sam. Doesn't she look lovely?"

Grace turned to see the boy hesitating in the doorway. He seemed insecure. She sensed it, and her heart swelled with love for the boy and his poor mother who had tried so hard.

Containing her overwhelming happiness wasn't easy but she didn't want to scare the lad. Gently she said, "Hi Sammy-son! I'll be proud to have you walk me down the aisle to meet your father. This is our day, for the three of us and we must all be involved. Right?"

"Right!" The boy ran forward, a joyous smile lighting his face. "Are you feeling much better now, Mummy?"

Grace knelt down in front of him and gathered his small body close. Her gown spread around the two, like an island of flowing white lace with them in the middle. Her veil, shielding them, shutting out the rest of the world. She hugged the lad and whispered. "I feel wonderful. And you, my son, look very debonair. I'm a lucky woman having two such handsome men in my life."

His voice lowered as he asked, "Are you happy now?"

"Yes, exceedingly happy. What about you, my son? Are you happy?"

"Y-yes."

"Sammy, what it is? There's something you're not telling me."

"Nanny says I'm not supposed to, and Daddy says I must wait a little longer."

"Look, we can solve whatever is bothering you, I promise."

"See, but you said so before and you forgot."

"My goodness, I know life has been hectic since I returned from the hospital, Sammy, but I'd never willingly forget something I've vowed to do. You must tell me what it is so we can correct my oversight." She kissed his cheek and peered into his face. That's when she saw his worry.

"Are you afraid I might get angry?"

He nodded.

"I promise I won't. Will that do? Do you trust me?"

His little arms snaked around her shoulders and he leaned closer to whisper in her ear.

"Oh, Sammy-son. As soon as Daddy and I get home from our honeymoon next week, we will make that happen." She put her hands over her heart and added, "I swear I won't forget this time, but you must make sure I don't. Okay?"

His face now glowing, the little chap nodded, "O-kay!"

"Now, shall we go and marry your father?"

"Yes!" He stuck out his arm and she put her hand there. Then she gathered the yards of her skirt and arranged them behind her so she wouldn't trip him or herself. Before they left the room, she picked up the gorgeous arrangement of mostly pink roses from the vase where they rested. Much earlier, Grace had insisted she wanted that particular flower in her bouquet and it heartened her to see that Lucas had remembered. After all, without the magic of a pink rose, she wouldn't be alive.

Music for the wedding march began to play as soon as they appeared at the entrance to the church. The first people Grace saw were her two wonderful friends, watching her carefully. She winked and they both clapped in delight. Henrietta's elbow knocked against Tobias with enough force that he had to grab for the pew in front to stop from being knocked over. Freddie stood with them and raised a hand in greeting and returned her wink.

The rest of the crowd was a blur. The only person who she saw from then on was the man waiting for her in front of the altar. He turned and watched her approach. His eyes were veiled and his expression somber.

She let Sammy lead her to his father. Before the ceremony could begin, she lifted her little boy into her arms, leaned in close to her husband and whispered, "I love you both, and I'll be the best mother and wife I can be. And, Lucas, just so we won't forget, I've promised we'll take Sammy shopping for his puppy the day after we return from our honeymoon."

Lucas jerked back and grabbed her face to lift toward his. He stared into the love shining from her eyes and his filled. "Thank God! My love, we'll go wherever your heart desires."

Another voice whispered in her head which made her happiness complete.

"And we'll be together—always!"

Afterword:

Thank you so much for reading *Together Always.*

I loved writing this story and I hope you enjoyed reading it. If so, I would ask you for a favor. Wherever you purchased this book, please take a few minutes and leave an honest review. Authors enjoy hearing that readers like their stories, and hopefully, others will see your words and choose to buy my work because of your sentiments.

My website at **http://mimibarbour.com** now has all my books listed with links to the various publishers to make it easy for you to return to where you bought the book and to find my other work.

While you're there, I'd really appreciate it if you would sign up for my newsletter so I can keep in touch.

http://bit.ly/mimibarbournewsletter

I only send out newsletters approximately twice a month. It's usually full of giveaways, contests and freebies along with my personal news. (You have my word that your address will never be shared.)

Hugs, Mimi

Together For Christmas

Vicarage Bench Series – Book #6

AMAZON (Free in Kindle Unlimited)

Is her spirit strong enough to win over the workaholic she's invaded?

Abbie Taylor has a thousand things to do before the big day, help the vicar with his needy families, organize the Christmas nativity, and spare time for a distraught baby at the orphanage who only settles when she's near. Falling into a coma while her spirit resides inside a prickly, big-shot businessman doesn't work for her at all... until she falls in love.

How could Marcus Chapman be so unlucky? First he's saddled with his newly widowed mum, and the next thing he knows, he has an annoying spirit invader who's instantly aware that he isn't nearly as tough as he makes out. Between these two manipulating women, and the orphans Abbie forces him to visit, the poor man doesn't stand a chance. The season is Christmas, and love is all around.

Chapter 1

Bury, England, 1969

"Sweet Jesus!"

Marcus Chapman shot to his feet. He'd thought himself alone when he sat on the bench in front of the old vicarage to analyse his disastrous day. *Must have dozed off*, he decided. The unexpected voice from behind the seat had not only woke him but also scared the hell out of him.

He leaned over the wooden back of the bench and stared down into shaggy bangs skimming over the widest and bluest eyes he'd ever seen. The girl kneeling there winced and tried a grin, which slowly faded when he refused to respond. She bowed her head, her grin changing to a grimace. Gathered on one side in a hair clip, masses of dark hair framed her pink cheeks and sparkled with some of the crystal flakes now steadily falling from the sky.

It was snowing. He looked around, astonished and disbelieving. This wasn't supposed to be happening today. The radio's morning report had promised colder temperatures, sure, but no one mentioned snow. *Goes to show why you should hardly ever pay attention to those misinforming blighters.*

His eyes felt heavy. *I must have fallen asleep.* When he'd first sat down, the sky had been overcast, and there had been a definite chill in the air. Now, however, fluffy flakes of white clung to branches like bits of tattered lace and had already covered most surfaces, including himself. Shivers attacked, and he lowered his body back onto the bench and wrapped his arms around his wet clothes. Heavy as his leather jacket was, when damp it didn't come close to warming him in the icy weather.

The girl's slight figure rose from behind the bench and stood, leaning toward him. "Sorry, mate. I didn't mean to disturb you."

"What are you doing, skulking behind this bench on your hands and knees? Are you hiding from someone?" With his teeth clacking, he sounded a bit comical.

She giggled, obviously thinking he was joking with her. He noticed she stopped when he didn't join in her merriment. At least she ended the annoying racket, but the devilment in her eyes spoke for itself. What a strange creature!

"I don't wish to intrude, but I'm trying to cover these rose bushes. I'm worried I didn't cut them short enough last fall when I trimmed them. I couldn't bear it if the weight of all this snow damaged their branches."

"It wasn't supposed to snow." His remark sounded petulant, but, dammit, snow hadn't been on the weather report. If he remembered correctly, they'd promised rain. In fact, he was sure of it, because he'd suffered a small twinge of remorse for his mother, who now lived with him—only until the repairs on her place were done, and not a minute longer. She'd been blathering on about a white Christmas for days.

He looked upward. "How long has it been falling?" The flakes were coming down so thickly it was difficult to see even as far as the vicarage close by.

"Blimey. It's been snowing steady for almost an hour, and it's gotten thicker as the time's passed. I've been going bonkers wondering whether to wake you or not. I knew you weren't dead, from the noise you were making. But when I saw the roses being overloaded, I realized I had to wrap them or take the chance on them dying from the cold."

She crouched down again and surveyed the area. Her short coat rode up and the hem of an even shorter skirt appeared, showing her well-formed legs in dark stockings and surprisingly large rubber boots. Silly girl will freeze in that outfit, he thought, before her voice grabbed his attention once again.

"Look here, I don't wish to annoy, but do you think you could help me with these sacks? Oops." She put her finger into her mouth, obviously having been pricked by one of the vicious thorns adorning the branches.

Her voice had a mesmerizing quality and, before he knew he intended to, he came around and reached for the side of the bag she held out to him. Again she smiled, and he watched as the rest of her face joined her lips to produce such a happy expression that he studied it bemusedly. She looked childlike, crouched so small, but he knew by her manner that she must have left school behind some time ago. A clearing of her throat and waving of the bag made him realize she still waited.

"Sorry." He spread out the edges she'd passed his way and leaned down to do his part.

"You're a good chap to help me. I appreciate it."

He could drown in the softness of her eyes. Still lost in what he'd seen there, he didn't pay attention. When she tugged on her end of the bag, he lost his balance. To keep from falling, he put out his hand, and it landed, palm down, on the closest bush. At first only the sting of the thorn piercing his skin registered. But then the girl's soft cry, hinting at a problem, caught his attention.

Dizziness, the first impression he noticed, prevailed and plunked him butt first into the snow. Then, befuddled, he watched as the girl across from him sighed, collapsed, and rolled over in what looked like a faint.

What the hell? *Breathe, you idiot, think and breathe. Stop this foolishness. Get to the girl. Call for help.*

His legs wouldn't hold him. *Right. Crawl, then, don't even try to stand.* Orders from a fuzzy brain rang in his head. Muddled and angry, he tried to force his body to obey the instructions, but it didn't work. Consciousness receded. A rushing sound overtook him and slammed him further from reality. Nausea attacked. His vision blurred. This time when he fell, he landed smack-dab on top of her.

After a few moments, life surged back into his frozen limbs. He opened his eyes and looked at the unmoving form under him. It took all his strength to roll over and another few seconds before he inched away. His rioting pulse slowed and erratic breathing returned to normal.

Struggling for coordination, he edged closer to the girl, loosened the blue silk scarf at her neck, and felt for a pulse. The beats seemed strong and normal, but when he checked her pupils—something he'd seen the doctors do on TV—there was no sign of life. The annoying ringing in his head continued until it crescendoed and then stopped. Eerie as it seemed, he blessed the quiet. His strength returned, and so did his equilibrium.

The girl still hadn't moved, and his concern grew. He needed to get her off the cold ground. Right now the closest warm place was the vicarage, where lights twinkled in the darkening shadows. Awkwardly, he swept her into his arms and began to struggle to his feet.

"What do you think you're doing?"

The shock of hearing her speak stunned him, and he dropped her. Her head lolled to the side, still lifeless. Damn, but he could have sworn she'd whispered the words he'd clearly heard. Feeling guilty for having let her go, he bent to lift her again.

"Am I dead?"

Disbelief had him backing off once more. "Excuse me?" Feeling rather foolish, he peered all around, trying to find a culprit who might sound like a corpse.

"I'm dead? I'm a corpse?" Her voice rose inside his head. *"Hold it. How can I be dead and still talk? You do hear me, don't you?"*

"No. Yes. I don't know. How can I hear you when you're mouth hasn't moved? In fact, nothing is moving on your body at all, except your pulse." Then he reached over to put his hand on her chest.

"Hey! What do you think you're doing?"

He whipped his hand back so fast he landed on his arse again. "Don't upset yourself. *I was merely feeling for a heartbeat."*

"What the... Think! If there's a pulse rate, surely I'd have a heartbeat?"

"How should I know that? I'm a businessman, not a doctor. This is absurd. You're out cold and we're carrying on this ridiculous conversation. I must be dreaming. This is impossible."

"Tell me about it. At least, you're moving. I'm staring down at my own body, and, I believe, I'm looking at it out of your eyes. Stone the crows! I am. Somehow I'm now inside of you. Must be an act of the supernatural."

"Quit this hysterical gibberish. How the devil can you be inside me?"

"Maybe 'cause we're carrying on a conversation without speaking? That might be a clue." He heard her sarcasm and didn't appreciate it at all.

"I do believe I'm dreaming. And when I wake up, you will be gone and—"

"You'll be frozen. So..."

"So what?"

"So, wake up, and let's stop this nightmare."

Marcus zippered his heavy sweater higher under his jacket, eased back up on his heels, and sighed.

"Well? What are you waiting for?"

"To wake up, of course."

"You are a dolt, aren't you?" The tug on his hair took him by surprise since he hadn't known he was going to be doing it.

"Ow! How did you do that?"

"I used your hand. S'truth, I'm lodged inside your body. If I can see from your eyes and use your hands, then I must be. It's the only thing that makes any sense. You're awake. You know it, and so do I."

Marcus swiped his shaking hand across his face to brush away the accumulated snow from his brows and eyelashes. He came to a decision. He'd make an appointment to see a psychiatrist as soon as possible. His hours had been brutal lately, what with moving to town and starting a new business, trying to do twenty things at once. No wonder he fell asleep while resting here. And no wonder he'd gotten caught up in these strange visions. This was obviously the result of overdoing things. Everyone knew stress played havoc with a tired mind.

Standing would require a bit of concentration. His legs felt rubbery, and the tingling warned him he'd been down on his knees far too long. Rose thorns tangled in his pant legs, and he lashed out at them.

"*Stop that. We're only just getting them back to health after some lunatic burnt them to the ground last year.*"

"*Sorry.*" He shuffled around the plant and grabbed the bench to help get to his feet.

"*Where do you think you're going?*"

"*To a hospital. I do believe I'm having some sort of a breakdown.*"

"*You're having a breakdown? Now you listen 'ere, Mate. It ain't you lying in a heap in the snow. And it darn well ain't you imprisoned in another's body, is it? Don't you dare try and leave me here.*"

Even if he wanted to, there was an unseen force holding him back—stopping him from moving. And, however unlikely, the girl certainly sounded real. Considering she was a figment of his imagination, that is.

"*Would you stop! I'm not a figment of anyone's imagination. I'm a real girl,*" she wailed. Then she added, "*Cor, I sound like the female version of Pinocchio.*" When she giggled, hysteria became evident.

"*Okay, stop that screeching. I'll take you with me.*" If this really was a dream, then he could play hero, even though he was far from hero material. Blast! How could a boring workaholic accountant such as himself get caught up in such a crazy nightmare?

Slight as she'd looked earlier, she felt solid to him now, and in his weakened condition, he knew he couldn't go very far. Scooped in his arms, her body rolled toward him as if seeking protection. He cradled her against his chest, and she seemed to fit. Strange. He'd never carried anyone before. He kind of liked how it made him feel.

He looked down and then lowered his chin so he could blow the snow from her features. Light from the lamp above angled over her, and he saw a small, heart-shaped face, pale and pretty, with lips plump and turning slightly blue.

"*See? I'm a girl.*"

"*Yes, I can see that now. Don't worry. I'll take care of you.*"

He stumbled out from behind the bench, stopped, and turned in both directions. The snow, falling even harder now, seemed to have effectively cleared the roads of traffic, both vehicular and human. No buses or taxis, no police or helpful pedestrians.

Again the lights from the vicarage drew his attention. The path, only slightly visible, wound through the gardens and looked to be a mile, when in truth he knew it to be only a couple hundred feet. Switching his romantic hold to that of a fireman, enabled him to keep one arm free as he headed in the right direction.

"*Do you have to carry me like a sack of potatoes?*"

"*It's easiest.*"

"*Don't blame me if I'm sick all over you. Upside down makes me dizzy.*"

He hurried. "*Don't you dare.*"

"*I'm glad you've decided to go to the vicar. He's my boss, you know, and a lovely chap. He'll know what to do, I'm sure.*"

"*Listen, I don't believe we should talk to anyone about your spirit—ahh—switching residences, so to speak. I mean, think about it. Would you accept such a thing? More than likely, if we try telling the truth, they'll stick me in a rubber room and throw away the key.*"

"*So, what do you propose we say about my unconscious body?*"

Strange how he not only heard the irritation, he felt her worry.

"*I'll tell him you stumbled and hit your head. We'll call an ambulance and get you taken to the hospital, where the doctors* can make an examination. *That oughta do it.*" Proud of his suggestion, he ignored her rude snort. Until she snorted the second time. "What??"

"*Have you looked around at all? There is no traffic. The roads look to be impassable. I'm afraid the storm is getting worse.*"

She had a point. The snow had intensified until visibility was almost nonexistent. If the foliage hadn't been protecting the biggest portion of this walkway from the blowing snow, he'd never be able to move so easily.

"*This is an emergency. They have to make it.*"

"*Pray God you're right.*" It was the sob that tore at the closed walls around his heart. A tiny sob, but with enough power to start the first fissure.

Vicarage Bench Series

The Vicarage Bench Series
Books 1, 2 & 3.

In **She's Me**, chubby, shy Lucy McGillicuddy who lives in a small English village in 1963 is forced to share herself with 2006 top model Jenna McBride. This experience teaches them both valuable lessons that enable them to finally accept true love.

In **He's Her**, schoolteacher Carrie Temple has to make space for Vegas casino owner Rhett Parks, whose spirit invades her heart as well as her mind, and won't leave. At first she desperately wants him to get out, but soon she can't bear for them to be apart.

In **We're One,** Vegas nightclub star Crystal Davis wants nothing to do with men until she's seduced by Ashley Parks while they flee from a killer. Ashley traps her spirit inside of him to keep her safe, but she soon convinces him to trust her—it's his safety they need to worry about.

About the author:

Mimi is an incredibly busy New York Times, USA Today and award-winning, best-selling romance author who has written seven series, including paranormal, contemporary and suspense. She also has numerous box collections and single titles to add to her credits.

Mimi lives on the East coast of Vancouver Island with her loving husband, and a son who makes her glad she was born a woman. Also a niece whose family adds greatly to her enjoyment of life. Gardening lights her inner fires, but alas, there's just not enough time to be outside when fictional characters vie to be heard.

Contact Information:

Amazon author page: http://bit.ly/MimiBarbourAmazon

My website: http://www.mimibarbour.com/

Or follow me on twitter: https://twitter.com/
MimiBarbour

Or on Facebook: Mimi Barbour Fan page

Please sign up for my fun Newsletter: http://bit.ly/
mimibarbournewsletter
or
Write to me anytime. I love to hear from my readers xo
mailto:mimibarbour66@gmail.com